PITHOLE

WHERE THE DEVIL DANCED

Robert Allen Pringle

ISBN: 978-1-63490-593-0

This novel is a work of fiction. All characters, companies, and creatures are fictional, any resemblance to real people are simply coincidental.

Pithole, Pa is a real historic site located in northwestern Venango County with a visitor's center and tours by accident.

Published by BookLocker.com, Inc., Bradenton, Florida, U.S.A.

Printed on acid-free paper.

BookLocker.com, Inc.
2015

First Edition

Dedication

For Mary, whose patience and quiet determination,
keep my feet on the ground.

In Memory of Sherri Lee Totty March 8th, 1973 - June 8th, 2015.
Rest in peace.

Acknowledgements

Big shout outs to Brenda Eldridge who keeps my "T"s dotted and my "I"s crossed, the kind and gracious ladies of the Sarah Stewart Bovard Memorial Library in Tionesta, Pa. who answer even the most mundane questions with a smile, and Mr. Ray Spangle, who believes in me.

Thank you all who helped make this book a reality. (If I were texting I'd put a smiley face here.)

Special Acknowledgement

All art work, including the outstanding cover, was done by Artist and Author, Debra Harrison whose suggestions and insight, are greatly appreciated. Not only is this lady talented and good looking, she's pretty darn smart too. Her children's book, "Creatures in my room" is a delight for child and parent alike.

Chapter One

Once, in the past, so far back as to be almost unimaginable, a tropical ocean covered the land I now sit upon, pecking away at my keyboard. In those vast primordial oceans life began, first with microscopic single cell creatures that absorbed their food directly from the molecules of the water. As millions of years passed they became more complex and after an epoch or two, (the amount of time ancient Earth biologists surmise that these changes occurred is staggering) they developed bodies and digestive systems, reproduction, sensory and mobility organs and limbs. They moved. They hunted.

What these biologists know is based on fossil records. They have studied only a tiny portion of solidified sea floor. They have only a rudimentary grasp of the evolution of life in the ocean. In reality, no one knows what creatures appeared, evolved, thrived and then went extinct in the billions of years of Earth's history.

Countless millions of species have called the oceans of this planet home only to vanish like a ripple in a wave on the surface, leaving no trace of ever having existed. What abilities, functions and intelligence levels these creatures or plants, for that matter had are unknown. We humans of the here and now consider ourselves the cutting edge of evolution yet we look at ancient anomalies and scratch our heads. Every day some new discovery is made by anthropologists of our past. Many are kept secret because they simply can't be explained by the accepted scientific view.

The geology of Earth is constantly changing. The estimated age of modern man's 100,000 years or so is merely the flick of a finger in the eons of time since the miracle of life occurred. Truly, we know next to nothing. The geological upheavals that occurred to form the sandstone and limestone caps that trapped the organic waste that became the coal and oil were spread out over eons of time.

When man arrived in western Pennsylvania, only the worn stumps of mountains that were greater than the Alps remained, with a scattering of glacial rocks lying silent in the vast hardwood forests. South of the great lake known as Erie, whose bottom was gouged out by two mile thick ice that moved undaunted in the great ice age, is the area known as the cradle of the oil industry.

Hundreds of years before Columbus, long before the fearless Norsemen plied the Atlantic Ocean braving the unknown. A group of people were building a mound in the shape of a serpent, in what is now Ohio. It was a rendition of their god. They called themselves the Children of the Snake. They would journey to the area later known as Penn's Woods, believing their great serpent lived beneath the soil there and its blood would collect on the surface in shining black pools.

They used the crude oil for medicine, paint and flaming sacrifice. Soaking the doomed animals and captives with it and then igniting it. They dug many pits to allow the oil to seep up and collect in a triangular area with the corners located at Franklin, Titusville and Tionesta. You can still find these pits today, if you wander deep into the woods.

When the Seneca Indians finally settled in the area, they found the same uses for the crude, except for the burning sacrifices. There was one area they avoided, where a gaping hole in the rocks gave off the odor of sulfur and seemed to have no bottom. No animals, birds or insects lived within a hundred feet of it, and mournful groans could be heard emanating from it on occasion.

Time passed, and white men appeared, stepping cautiously around the ancient trees, avoiding the natives while exploring the land. The French descended from Canada, plying the rivers, meeting the Indians, trading with them and befriending them. Wars were fought, but the westward push of the relentless white man could not be stemmed. The innocuous valley waited in silence for the sound of the axe.

In the east the inhabitants rebelled against their king, but only faint echoes of their battles ever reached the verdant hills. Against all odds, the rebels persevered and in gratitude to the troops all were granted land of their choice west of the Appalachian Mountains.

In 1787 a group of three men entered the valley, following the small creek that flowed into the Allegheny River. One of them caught a whiff of the sulfur fumes, and they went to investigate. Sulfur was necessary in the making of gun powder, which was always in short supply in the wilderness.

They passed by a pit with a stinking pool of black liquid gathered in it, with nothing growing where it touched the ground. They topped a small rise, and saw what they thought was a cave in a group of rocks. They also noticed the absolute quiet of the immediate area. In the forest there is a constant sound of life, insects buzzing, birds chirping and small game moving about. Here, silence, like the grave.

The smell seemed to be coming from the dark opening, and the youngest of them gave his musket to his friend and went to investigate. A slight breeze blew at his back as he got on his knees to peer into the hole. He inadvertently knocked a few stones in, and they made slight noises as they bounced and fell. Deep in the abysmal cavern a pair of eyes, black as obsidian, opened and gleamed.

The wind abated for a few seconds, and the fumes from inside overcame the curious teenager, and he was rendered unconscious. When he didn't respond to the others calls they rushed down to help him. They dragged him away from the opening, and in a few minutes he came to. He was shouldering his pack when he saw the man standing on the rise above them.

At first they thought he was a preacher. Dressed all in black, an ankle length duster, and a flat brimmed round hat, but his ear to ear grin was unsettling. Long jet black hair down to his shoulders, and shining black eyes, he stood with his hands held out to his sides. The three woodsmen stared and felt uneasy. The man raised his hands, leaves and twigs began to swirl in the air on both sides of him. The eldest of them shouted "Devil", raised his musket and fired. The man simply laughed in a voice that was too loud, and leapt at them. Their screams echoed unheard through the forest for hours.

Time passed, and more people came to the area. The towns of Franklin, Titusville and Tionesta prospered. Many more took to farming, claiming the uninhabited land. On a homestead lot beside an unnamed creek, a Mr. Holmren cleared some forest and built a home. He continued to clear the trees away, but the soil was poor with many rocks. His wife and three children toiled beside him in his endeavor to eke out a very modest living.

The forest was rich in game however, and they ate reasonably well with deer and turkey as their staples. There was an occasional bear as well. To the east near Titusville, a determined man named Drake worked hard to find a salt deposit he was sure lay under the ground. He fashioned a drilling device using a steam engine, which hammered a steel rod down into the ground. He never found the salt he sought. He discovered oil instead.

A new industry arose, with wild eyed speculators, cash in hand, competing for oil rich sites. Derricks rose, displacing the aged trees, and money was made. The seekers of fortune began to range out in all directions, and new towns sprang to life, Oil City, Oileopolis, Rouseville to name a few. All prospered as the oil boom took hold.

In the summer of 1864, a year after the carnage of Gettysburg, with the civil war still going strong, laborers were scarce. Speculators were still abundant however, and one morning two men appeared at the Holmren farm. After a brief discussion, they were permitted to look over the property for possible drilling sites. One of the men had a forked witch hazel stick he called a divining rod. He held it out in front of himself, grasping the two forks loosely in his fingers and began to wander around.

The branch pulled him in a certain direction, until he came to a round depression in the ground. The stick dipped so hard and quick it stuck in the ground right in the middle of the pithole. The other man remarked how lucky they were, as they wouldn't have to dig a pit to begin with. Terms were discussed with Mr. Holmren, and he agreed to lease the land for five years, for fifty thousand dollars. All buildings on the site at that time reverted to him, and he received twenty five percent of all oil discovered. The speculator walked away happy, with a lease for two hundred acres in his vest pocket.

Within a week a derrick was set up, and a spudder drill operating. Two hundred feet and some traces of oil were found in the first sand layer. Punching through rock at four hundred feet they found more traces in the second sand, after five hundred feet, nothing, six hundred feet, nothing. At seven hundred, an especially hard layer of rock was encountered. Progress was slow, and prospects looked weak. The decision was made to keep pounding down for fifty more feet.

The next day they broke through the bedrock, and oil began to flow. The immense underground pressure forced the oil up the shaft at an astounding rate of a hundred barrels a day, with the hole still plugged with the drilling tools. Every able bodied man dug a holding pit, but the oil increased its flow. They filled barrels as fast as they could get them.

News of the strike went out, and within a week over a thousand men were there, leasing plots and drilling more wells. A town was staked out, and lots sold, with the understanding that in five years all land and buildings would become the property of farmer Holmren. The boom was on.

The original well, now named the United States well, was unplugged and the oil flowed at the rate of twelve hundred barrels a day, a new record. Leases sold for up to a hundred thousand dollars cash. Five thousand men now swarmed on the property, with more arriving daily. Rough roads were cut, and soon became muddy morasses. An unbroken line of teamsters, hauling five barrels each, stretched from the new town of Pithole to Titusville, a distance of fifteen miles. They had to cut down an untold number of young trees to build a corduroy road, it was like a rough washboard most of the way. Horses and mules were worked to death, and their rotting carcasses lined the ungodly road.

Buildings sprang up seemingly overnight. One hotel, accommodating a hundred and twenty guests was built in one day! Taverns and brothels were slapped together, and immediately opened for business. In the midst of the noisy hubbub, few people noticed a man dressed all in black, who walked up and down, with a wide grin fixed on his swarthy face. He would enter the drinking establishments and stand to one end of the bar, observing the riotous men and the dancing girls. He took an interest in one young man, a handsome actor trying his hand on speculation by the name of John Wilkes Booth, and was seen in deep conversation with him.

The gamblers came, the confidence men, the thieves, crooks and bullies. Among them a bare knuckled brawler named Ben Hogan, who called himself the wickedest man on earth. He held up ten thousand dollars in cash, and said he'd fight any man if he could put up the money. The crew at the Deep Molly well put up the cash, and the fighter, Big Dick McGuire. Dick weighed three hundred pounds, a solid mass of tough Irish muscle, and a popular fellow in the town. Hogan, at six foot even, and one hundred eighty pounds, had his work cut out.

That evening, the other men put up a makeshift ring right on Holmren Street, and the fight was on. Bare knuckles and no rules, the two men went at it. Hogan's' attack was so fast and vicious that big Dick only hit him once. Within two minutes, McGuire was on his back in the filthy dirt, his face battered and bleeding. The onlookers stood mute, stunned.

Hogan took his winnings and opened a bar beside French Kate's' Gentlemen's Sporting House, and the two got along well. Hogan proved to be a braggart, bully, and just plain disagreeable. Then one night it was raining like hell out, and Ben was alone in his bar, where he served warm beer and moldy cheese. The door opened, and the man in black entered. Rain blew in on the hemlock floor, but the grinning man was bone dry.

"Evening", he said with his customary wide grin, "not busy I see."

"You want something or what?" Hogan said belligerently.

"Oh I just wanted you to know that you are not the wickedest man on earth." His black eyes sparkled in the oil lamp light as he spoke. Hogan watched amazed as the man's head changed shape to that of a snake, the grin widening with a row of razor sharp teeth. A forked tongue flicked out and he hissed, "I am."

The next day the bar was deserted. There were so many transients, that no one noticed when someone wasn't there the next day. People would just shrug, and go back to making and spending money. French Kate immediately took it over and expanded her enterprise. Hogan was forgotten.

One month later he was seen speaking at a temperance meeting in Cleveland. He carried a Bible with him everywhere, and had sworn off drink forever. His hands trembled as he spoke in halting terms.

"Drink brought me face to face with Satan himself, the evil serpent. Why I still live I'll never know, but I will never touch another drop again." Sometimes breaking a man's pride is worse than killing him.

In the boomtown there was no law to speak of, except public opinion, and that was pretty low. Pithole was red hot, open for business twenty four hours a day, every day. Only the grocery stores were closed on Sundays. A store on Holmren Street went up for sale one morning for two thousand dollars. By five o'clock, it sold for the fifth time for sixty thousand. The brothels all had one special room where two exhausted girls could sleep for four hours at a turn.

In a shack behind French Kate's' Sporting House, a young woman was found dead, with most of her lower stomach missing, outside in the mud, the headless body of a new born lay. Two feet of the umbilical cord, still attached and bitten off.

The teamsters kept raising their rates until there were only pennies to be made on a barrel, but the oil kept flowing. The barrel coopers had to transport wood from farther and farther away. Firewood used to heat the water for the steam engines became scarce and the price for it rose. The local game was gone and the expense of eating every day increased. The teamsters grew more aggressive and demanding. Then a feller got an idea and built a pipeline, the first of its kind. They ran the pipe down Pithole Creek to the Allegheny where barges lined up and filled 1000 gallon tanks to be floated on down river to Reno to be refined. They only wanted the kerosene and heavier lubricants. They dumped the waste right into the Allegheny, what would later be known as gasoline and diesel fuel. On the pipeline, they had to post armed guards every fifty feet to keep the teamsters from disrupting the flow. The threat of fire was great, the very ground was saturated with crude oil and chunks of paraffin wax lay scattered about.

Many large signs were erected saying, "NO SMOKING", "NO OPEN FIRES". With all the disruption to the subsurface, the water wells would sometimes turn to crude. So much was spilt by accident or just poor control of the volume, the creek was lined with people skimming oil off the surface with buckets and filling their own barrels.

Then fire broke out at what was known as the twin wells. Men manned the pumps until the water turned to oil and added to the conflagration. Great wooden holding tanks, containing up to twenty thousand gallons, burst into flames and collapsed, the burning liquid flooding the streets, engulfing man and horse alike. In the middle of all this raging hell, the man dressed in black was seen howling out laughter as he danced along the way, the flames not touching him. In the morning Pithole was a smoking ruin.

The hotel survived as well as a few other structures, but the building was torn down and the salvaged boards were used to build a house in Titusville, now the historical home of Ida Tarbell.

Most of the survivors left, but a few stalwart souls tried to rebuild the burnt derricks and shacks. The oil petered out in a couple years and soon the last wagon left searching for new prosperity. The area was an ecological disaster. It would be many years before Mother Nature began to heal the scars. Farmer Holmren loaded his belongings and abandoned his farm, whistling as he went.

Chapter Two

In 1972, Venango County which had acquired Pithole for the total sum of four dollars and thirty seven cents back in 1867 was informed by the state that they were going to build a memorial museum close to the site. It was July and hot. Construction was well underway, and by two in the afternoon, most of the workers were shirtless and sweating as they lay the cement blocks erecting the walls. The building was situated on a rise just off the gravel road that gave access to the farms nearby. The valley where the streets were still discernable in the overgrown fields lay below the future tourist destination.

One of the young men stood up and wiped his forearm across his sweaty brow and noticed a figure approaching from the former Holmren farmstead. It was a man dressed all in black, wearing a full length coat, a wide brimmed preacher's hat and heavy boots.

"Howdy boys," he greeted them with a wide grin, "what in the world are you doing?"

The foreman replied as the men took a quick water break. He told the man about the state and the museum. They noticed that even with the heavy clothes the man was not perspiring or even seemed uncomfortable in the ninety degree heat and smothering humidity. He even had on black leather gloves.

"Oh good," he exclaimed, "then people will come back around. I can't wait." He then tilted his head back and began to laugh out loud. He turned and walked back towards the empty fields away from the astonished workers.

"I'll be damned," said the foreman.

The man, who was now a couple hundred feet away stopped and looked back, still with that incredible grin on his face, he laughed once more and all the men plainly heard him say, "You probably are." Then he vanished in thin air.

--- --- --- --- --- --- --- ---

June ninth, 1974. Bill Lyons was washing his '71 Roadrunner in his driveway. He had a date later on that evening with pretty Patty Tatem. The music coming from the eight track tape player was a new Led Zepplin album, and it was hot!

Things were going good for young Bill. He had a job pumping gas, the car ran great and he was probably going to get laid tonight. He had a case of Pabst on ice in the trunk just to make things easier. Jerry, the mechanic at the station had gotten it for him. He was just hosing it off, when his mom came out on the porch and called him to dinner.

Patty was trying to decide between shorts or the mini skirt. There was a new song on the radio by a band called Foghat, and ohhh did it make her want to dance. Billy might get laid tonight, she thought, but first we're gonna talk about getting married. She put on the mini.

Her dad was giving her a ration of shit about the way she was dressed, just when Bill pulled in the drive. She told her dad she was eighteen now and would dress as she damned well pleased. The screen door slammed shut as she headed for the car. They took off and headed for Titusville and the main street drag where everybody with a hot car would cruise up and down waving at friends and goosing their engines.

Bill didn't want to be doing this long as gas had just gone up to the unbelievable price of 49.9, damn Arabs. Patty was pouting as he turned east on 36 and opened up the four barrel on his 440. She had to admit to herself she loved it when the power surge pushed her back in the bucket seat. He cranked the tunes, J Giles with Magic Dick on the licking stick.

They turned off on Pithole road and he stopped and got a couple cans of beer out of the trunk, pulled the rings and peeled back the little tear shaped tabs. "About time," said Patty, taking a long sip. They drove out past the museum to a lane leading into the woods. He drove back in and parked. It was growing dark, and Bill got a blanket out of the backseat, handed it to Patty and went and gathered some firewood. He opened the trunk and got a couple more brews. Patty was busy rolling a joint, careful not to spill any. Pot was expensive now, $25.00 an ounce.

Bill had the Stone's Sticky Fingers tape in and they joked and partied for a little while then Patty got down to business. She took his hand, leaned in and kissed him, "Bill, what do you think about marriage?"

He looked at her like she was joking but then realized she was serious. "Uh, marriage, yes, well, it uh, seems to work for some folks."

"Yes, yes it does," gushed Patty, "I could get a job somewhere and we could buy a house and..."

"Whoa, slow down a little here. I pump gas for two bucks an hour. Just maybe enough to rent a place if we find a cheap one."

"Oh you'll find a better job and aren't you learning how to work on cars now? It would be nice, and then we can do this whenever we want." She reached to kiss him and they laid back. The mini came in handy after all.

In the shadows beyond the campfire light the man in black was almost invisible. His eyes gleamed as he watched the busy couple, his wide grin a testament to his enjoyment. He raised his hands as the couple reached their climax and a gust of misty wind blew over them.

Nine months later Patty presented her husband with a beautiful, delicate baby girl they named Jessie Jayne. Bill had remembered the pot and the beer, but forgot about condoms. He had gotten a better job at Square Deal Tire and Lube, (square deals on round tires was their motto). Patty volunteered to help at the courthouse with elections and got a job helping Joe Whitlock in his bid for congress.

They bought an old camp with a 1950's something trailer on it at the tax sale. It was only a couple miles outside Tionesta. Patty's mother had a lot to do with that in more ways than one. She worked at the courthouse and put up half the money. Bill's dad helped him fix it up a bit and with some used furniture donations from family and friends they had a nice little place.

The Roadrunner was gone but they had a good, solid four wheel drive Chevy truck. They needed it as the road they lived on got no winter maintenance from the township. Boondocks, is a word that comes to mind.

The nearest neighbor was a half mile away but they were comfortable with that. The baby was healthy and happy, life wasn't bad.

About two years passed and one afternoon in late spring Patty had Jessie outside playing with a large plastic ball when a man came walking up the road. Patty saw the stranger all dressed in black with a wide brimmed circular hat and a full length coat, stop on the road in front of the house.

"Mighty fine day Ma'am, mighty fine day," he said in greeting, "might I ask for a glass of water?"

She glanced at her daughter and the man said, "I'll keep an eye on her", as a happy grin spread across his face.

"I'll be right back", Patty said with authority and walked briskly into the house. She returned a minute later with a Tweety Bird glass they had got at McDonald's. The man had advanced only a step or two to the edge of the lawn. He nodded his thanks, but his grin made Patty uneasy.

"My husband will be home from work real soon," she stated flatly.

He was gazing at the baby who was pulling bits of grass up and putting them in her mouth. "A beautiful child you have there and so healthy looking also."

"Yes, she is a blessing," Patty replied.

With that the man laughed out loud and handed the glass back. She noticed there were bits of ice in it now. He put his hand to the brim of his odd hat still with that wide grin plastered on his face and turned. "It was a pleasure, such a nice baby." He walked away. She watched him disappear around the bend and noticed he hadn't touched a drop of the water.

Bill listened carefully to her account of the encounter over a dinner of fish sticks and tater tots. He sat there and thought for a little while then sighed. "I've been a fool," he told his wife and went outside to the all purpose shed slash workshop out back. He returned carrying something wrapped in an old towel.

"What's that," she asked?

"Protection, I don't know why I didn't do this sooner." He revealed a chrome plated .38 revolver. "I sorta forgot about it."

"Forgot about it, how long has it been out there?" she couldn't believe it, they didn't have too many secrets between them, none as of yet, anyways.

"You remember back when I found that skull on the game lands this side of Pithole?"

"Yeah, you were what, fourteen, fifteen?" Patty was looking concerned.

"Thirteen, the gun was laying there in the leaves. I wanted it and never told the cops," Bill said with a shrug.

"Oh my God Bill, that is evidence. They had a murder investigation. That could have solved a crime!"

"Suicide's more like it, who would have marched some guy a mile and a half into the woods to put a bullet in his brain? Anyway you're gonna learn how to shoot it."

Patty looked at him and then looked at the gun, she was intrigued. The only weapon she ever fired before was an old .22 her dad had. She really liked the cop shows on TV, especially Cagney and Lacy, she favored Cagney. The baby was watching them from the highchair, eyes wide and her mouth open in a little "o".

"Okay, when?"

"I'll pick up a couple boxes of shells on payday, you can set some bottles and cans up on those rocks behind the shed," Bill said.

Patty looked up at him, "Hey, they ever figure out who that guy was?"

"Nope, they only found a few bones and the guy didn't have any teeth. No wallet, no shoes, no keys or coins, just that skull with two holes in it. The funny thing I found out was all the shells were fired, he musta saved the last one for himself."

Patty shrugged and picked up the gun, the baby began to cry.

Chapter Three

Over the Fourth of July the area was pretty crowded. All kinds of people were visiting, vacationing and such. Canoe trips down the Allegheny were popular and pup tents sprang up like mushrooms around a cow plat. The Fourth happened to fall on Monday that year and Bill had two days off in a row. One of his buddies had ran over to Ohio and loaded up on fireworks and they were gonna have a kegger. Patty's sister Tina was coming with her three boys and maybe her husband, (there was a little friction there). They looked for about twenty people in all.

Patty's mom came early in the morning and they were cooking up mac and potato salad. Bill's mom and dad were coming and bringing some chairs from the church. Bill and his father in law had gone to get the beer and ice. Bill still wasn't old enough to buy it legally in Pennsylvania. The baby, two and a half now, was busy with her toys on the living room floor.

"So," Patty's mom Laverne asked, "when are you two gonna have me another grandbaby?"

"We're working on it Mom," Patty laughed, "hard at work."

"I bet," her mom giggled as she poured steaming macaroni in a colander. Laverne had brought her famous Waldorf salad that everyone called "elf snot" and it was in the old fridge. They chatted some more, spreading out the gossip as the potatoes cooked. Patty glanced in the living room. "Mom, where's the baby?"

The room was empty. They quickly got up and started looking. Little Jessie wasn't in the house; she had wandered outside and was on the grass playing with something. The women went out to get her and froze. There was a huge blacksnake coiled between the child's legs, what was called a blue racer. Jessie was petting it like a puppy, it could bite but wasn't poisonous.

Laverne got the broom and whispered to Patty to get ready to grab Jessie. She carefully got the straw end close to the snake's head. It noticed, raised back and hissed. "NOW!" she jammed the straw into the snake's mouth, pushing the head back and Patty lifted the toddler out of the way. The serpent struck at the broom, then fled as fast as it could go. The baby was howling.

"Is the baby alright? Is the baby alright?" Laverne asked as goose bumps danced on her arms.

"Yes Mom she's fine," Patty said with relief, "she's just taken a fright is all."

"Oh my God, thank you Jesus," Laverne had tears in her eyes, "I was so scared."

"Well no harm done Mom, how's about a drink, I could sure use one right about now." Patty said and swung back to the house. Laverne just looked at her.

Patty was mixing rum and cokes when the men got back. They told the tale and Bill and Buddy got shovels and searched the yard, no snake.

"Well Laverne," Buddy said, "you musta scared it off. It's gone now."

Bill went over and picked up Jessie and held her, she was getting sleepy. The women took her in for a nap and the men got the keg set up, and what the heck tapped it. The ladies came back out with their Looney Toons glasses and a car pulled in.

"Oh wow, they brought Lulu Lava," Patty laughed, "watch out Dad, she'll eat you alive."

Bill's buddies John and Jimmy Ward got out along with this sassy lady with wild blonde hair. Bill always thought she was the spitting image of Janus Joplin with bigger boobs.

"Look who we picked up," Jimmy said with a smirk.

Lulu cocked her hip, "Picked up? These two good looking men came and groveled on their knees begging, pleading for me to come with them. I felt sorry for them even though I could have stayed home listening to Jerry Falwell and watching my mother crochet."

"Hi Lulu," Patty giggled, "there's beer or do you want a ladies drink?"

"Wow, you got the Tasmanian Devil glass? You know me." They went in.

The men all filled their mason jars and started talked about snakes.

"Yeah," said Jimmy, "me and John here were going through the woods out behind Pithole one day, you never know what you'll find out there. Anyways we're walking along looking when John puts his hand out and stops me, then he starts backing up, pushing me. I say's what and he points up. There musta been two hundred big ass blacksnakes hanging off'n the tree branches. We almost walked under them."

"Scared the shit outta me," John muttered, a long sentence for him. Jimmy made up for him though, always talking.

"Then what'd you do," asked Buddy.

"Do? Shit, we got the hell outta there, what'da ya think?" Jimmy nodded at all the other men.

"Weird shit down in those woods," Bill said, "always was."

"Yeah, I heard stories too," Buddy added.

Just then a beat up old Dodge van pulled in and a cloud of smoke rolled out when the folks inside stumbled out. They were all saying hello and filling glasses when Bill's Mom and Dad drove up in their big ass Chrysler. Bill lit the fire and the younger fellas went to cut sticks. That's when Tina showed up with her tribe, less one husband.

The ladies all helped to set out the goodies and paper plates and such. There's a delicate art to roasting hot dogs on a stick. Not too close, not too far away. You want 'em just a little crispy and if a little bit of ash gets on it oh what the heck, that's what mustard is for.

It was a pleasant afternoon, Lulu cracking jokes, the kids playing nice, the beer was cold. They set a tent up for the boys and after dark came the fireworks. They fired them off to the oohs and awes. The keg got kicked and the van people left for wetter parties. That's when John Ward opened his trunk and got out two cases of Bud. Both sets of parents went home, and the party slowed down to a comfortable roar.

Lulu looked up and said, "Patty, you hear anything about some cult moving into the old Yoder place?"

"Yeah, Mom said they applied for tax free status as a church, 'bout ten or eleven of 'em", Patty nodded her head.

"No shit, what kinda church?" asked Jimmy.

Tina spoke up, "I heard they were devil people, uh... you know, Satanists, yeah, Satanists."

"Maybe they're what's left of the Manson Family." Bill interjected and made a scary noise.

"Jehovah Witnesses, if you ask me," John muttered. They all just looked at him. "What? We could go spy on them."

"You can go spy on a bunch of Satanic Jehovah Witlessess if you want to John boy, I'm rolling another doobie," and Lulu bent to the task.

They were up to the wee hours, Tina crawled in with her boys, the Ward brothers slept in their car and Lulu got the couch of honor. Sunday morning Jessie Jayne, (who needed her night diaper changed) was staring at Lulu sleeping on the couch. She had found the bowl of left over mac salad in the fridge and it was smeared on her face, in her hair and there was a little trail of it from the refrigerator to the couch.

She decided Lulu looked hungry and dropped some elbows in her open mouth. Lulu lunged up sputtering and yelling, the child started wailing and dropped what was left of the salad on the carpet. Patty came rushing out in her night shirt and stepped on the cold, slippery mess with her bare foot and let out a whoop as she landed on her butt. It had been so quiet. Later it was funny.

Three months later a visitor to the old Yoder place found the place deserted. A meal had been half eaten on the table, the closets and drawers were full of clothing and many personal objects were cluttered about. It was like they all walked out in the middle of dinner and never returned. No trace of the people was ever found. Folks stayed away from the place.

....

Time passed, Jessie started school and Patty got her own car, a used Dart, to drive Jessie to the bus stop. Patty's Dad died of a heart attack and they sold their place and moved in with Patty's Mom. There was a nice insurance check and with the money they got from the old camp Bill decided to go into business for his self.

He had his tools and the state inspection license. They added two bays to Dad's garage, putting a hydraulic lift in one of them. He traveled up to Buffalo, and brought back a used four wheel drive wrecker. They fixed up an office with an old metal desk and a couple coats of paint. The place sat along route 36 just inside the Forest County line. Patty's sister painted them a nice sign and they were in business.

Jessie was growing like a bad weed, endlessly curious and interested in everything, she was a darn good kid. Patty kept the books in order, did what advertising they could afford, and found she had a natural talent for it. Bill got a repair account with the state police and hired his old buddy Woody, part time at first, but business grew along with his reputation.

One day during archery season the phone rang. The state police needed a four wheel drive wrecker off Pithole road. Bill showed up a little while later, and was pointed down the same lane where he and Patty had dallied back a few years ago.

He had to drive up in the brush to get by a cruiser parked in the way but figured that's what 4WD was for. There was a late model Jeep Cherokee parked, with an officer who was looking in the backseat. Another policeman was standing at the rear writing on a legal pad. Bill set his brake, got out and walked over to him.

"Hey Bill," said officer Banks, "got us an abandoned vehicle here but we want it held secured"

"Sure, I'll lock it up in the inspection bay unless you guys want it up on a lift." Bill said as he opened his work order and began to fill it out.

"No, I think just seal it for now. Looks like a missing person, hunter, his wife called in, said he's two days overdue. We're calling in a search team, fire department, helicopter if we need it. We'll find him."

The other officer came over, "Nothing in the car looks suspicious, got some hunting stuff but no notes, and no signs of foul play."

Officer Banks nodded, "Okay Bill, we'll get out of your way. I'll follow you in." Both of them got in the cruiser and backed out the lane.

Bill maneuvered around and hooked it up. When they all got back to the garage Bill backed it in the bay and unhooked it. Officer Banks put white tape on the doors, sealing them off. Bill closed the bay door and secured it, then went out the man door and locked it as well.

On the third day of the search they found him. He was dead, fifteen feet up in the fork of a cherry tree. His right arm and left leg were missing. They had walked right underneath him on the first day, and only saw him because of a crow pecking at his eye and flapping its wings.

The investigators were stumped. There were no marks on the tree where someone would have climbed up to place the body there. There were no blood stains on the tree or on the ground underneath. One observer made the remark that it appeared that the body had been thrown up there. The man received several sideways glances. They did not find the missing limbs or any hunting equipment.

The body was collected by the Venango County Coroner with much difficulty. They had to climb up and rig a sling to lower the dead man down, and then carry the corpse out.

The deceased, Mr. James Winger of Youngstown, Ohio had been 41 years old with a wife and family. There was nothing in his background to suggest anything other than a steady man who had a steady job.

Detective Brian McMasters and his partner, Detective David Sike were assigned. Sike was the rookie, sort of, after ten years of patrol duty and some night classes, he got promoted. This was his first case as a detective. The coroner's report stated the cause of death as massive blood loss. The arm had been wrenched from its socket and the muscle tissue ripped. The leg bone had been broken at mid-thigh and again the muscles ripped with great force. The body had been placed in the position of its discovery three to four hours after death. How it had been placed remained a mystery.

A forensics team went over the Jeep but found nothing out of place. It was released to the man's widow. She sold it to Bill she didn't even want to look at it.

The detectives were at a loss, the only animal capable of doing the acts committed would have been a great ape and the odds that one had been in the area were close to zero. Imagining a man being able to rip another man's arm and leg off, carry him an undetermined distance and throw two hundred pounds of dead meat fifteen feet in the air was preposterous. The case went unsolved.

Chapter Four

Summer! Glorious summer! School was out and for twelve year old Jessie Jayne it was the best of times. There was a path across the field behind her place that led to her best'est friend Mary Bowser's house and she was on her bike pedaling that way now. When she got there she said, "Hi" to Mary's mom and the two girls went to their "mansion".

It was an old pump station for a former oil lease, with the huge iron motor still there. They had fixed it up some with a card table and an old set of chairs, a dented steamer trunk that had a faint scent of mothballs, and a makeshift bookshelf.

Both girls had a few "Seventeen" and "Teen beat" music magazines and would pour over them relentlessly. When it rained the noise was loud on the thin tin roof, but it only leaked in a few spots. They played "Star Trek" in there, voyaging to strange new planets, and meeting good looking alien boys. They discussed boys, training bras, menstrual stuff, boys, school friends, bullies, bitchy teachers and boys.

Mary's thirteenth birthday was coming up, and she was allowed to invite who she wished, certain girl friends of course, but which boys? It was that wonderful, horrible time of coming to age when a small faux pas or a pimple in the wrong place could be devastating. After much debate and giggling, they finally agreed on which boys they dared to invite. The birthday party was considered a success, with a long game of spin the bottle and post office combined.

About three weeks later they were bored. They put down the magazine with the "New Kids on the Block" pictures and decided to go for a walk. Wearing cheap sneaks, shorts and t-shirts they got a canteen of water, a pack of gum and a couple stout sticks. They followed a thin path they knew into the woods. Mary led the way and after a while said, "My Grammy said to stay out of this place. She said the devil dances out here, but my Dad said he's too busy everywhere else to be bothered with this old forgotten place."

Just then they spooked a quail, which in turn startled them in the blast of sound and feathers when it bolted from its hiding place.

They looked at each other and laughed. "Everybody says this patch of the forest from here to old Pithole is spooky," Mary said, "hard to imagine there was fifteen thousand people here, all running around drilling for oil." Jessie swung her stick at a sad looking fern, "Yeah, but they ain't drilling for crap now, are they?"

They came upon a huge uprooted tree, its roots lifting a twenty foot circle of dirt straight up. They stopped to examine it. Rocks, roots, dirt, wait! "Look," said Mary, "what's that?" It looked like a little chunk of pipe. Jessie grabbed hold of it and yanked, it was stuck. They poked around with their sticks and pulled on it again, this time it fell out.

"Wow! Look," Jessie exclaimed, "it's some kinda old gun or something." They cleaned the dirt and debris off it and found what must have been a trigger mechanism on one end. They looked hard at the rest of the dirt caught in the roots and the hole that was there, but didn't find anything else.

"We'll take this to my dad," said Mary, "he'll know what it is."

"Okay," Jessie said, "but we'll keep this place quiet and come back with shovels and stuff. We may find some old coins and gold rings, or other stuff."

"Yeah, I bet this is where some pioneer got scalped, or there was a big battle. We can find all kinds of things, maybe even a skull." They never noticed the black snake that was coiled and watching them from the ferns.

The girls carried their treasure out of the woods and took it to Mary's house, where her mom sprayed it off with a hose. They all waited for Mary's dad to get home from work. Her dad looked at it for a little while, and then called Jerry Hanson who was a gunsmith. He came out to take a look and pronounced it an antique. He convinced the girls to let him take it home to his shop where he would clean it some more and maybe identify it.

Two days later he returned it and told them it was a revolutionary war era musket, a British Brown Bess. It could have been seized by the owner from a redcoat in a battle. It wasn't loaded. The girls couldn't believe their ears.

They got their picture in the Forest Press holding the long barrel. A man came from the college in Titusville and wanted to see where they had found it. While he was there, he wandered about a little and examined a large hole in a group of piled up rocks not very far away. He tossed a rock in and never heard it touch bottom, he turned and left.

There was talk at the drinking establishments about how that gun came to be there, and most of the conclusions ended up as an unfortunate incident for the man who was carrying it. Jessie's granddad took a special interest in it, and carved a new stock and barrel piece for it. Since both girls owned it and couldn't decide which house to display it at, they took it to the local historical society and let them display it.

It was a time of prosperity for the Lyons family. Bill landed a contract with the county and hired a truck mechanic. Patty took an interest in local politics and began attending meetings and events. Soon she was back volunteering to help in campaigns and voter awareness, and then she ran for and got elected as a county representative.

Jessie was doing well in middle school. She wasn't in the glamour clic, and much preferred jeans to skirts. Somewhat athletic, she tried out for and was surprised when she made JV cheerleader. She had boyfriends of course, but nothing serious beyond holding hands and daring kisses.

The spring after her fifteenth birthday her dad started to teach her how to drive. She got to learn the old dirt roads well. The Jeep Bill had bought so long ago had been kept garaged all this time and was now designated for Jessie. She loved it, there was only eighteen thousand miles on it and ran like it was new.

*****

Deep underground not far from the Lyons residence, a ripple ran through the immense body. Trapped for millennia it had given up on finding a way out of the confining space and contented itself with the avatars it could project to the surface. It had soon learned that it could sustain itself on the energy released by the death of the prey it took, through the channeled energy used to create the images it hunted with.

In the distant past, it had entered the cavern to hibernate due to the intense cold of a long forgotten ice age. At that time, a rare earthquake occurred and the rocks shifted, trapping it in a pocket of brine water. It longed for the taste of real flesh and blood, the satisfying feeling of a full stomach, even the release of waste. It had mated just before the cataclysm that had trapped it and that cycle was suspended as well as all of its bodily functions. The creature had a high level of intelligence also and if its kind had been allowed to evolve would probably had been the dominate species on Earth. Mother Nature is fickle however.

In the modern era its favorite avatars were the blacksnake and for the past few thousand years, man. It had such jolly fun as a human, especially the one it used now. When the energy field it commanded projecting an image made contact with a living creature, the avatar became solid and then could kill, absorbing the life force of its victim. It had been one of nature's perfect accidents of creation, not only being able to sustain itself two different ways, but also able to wait until food was available. Adapted to either the vast oceans of Earth or dry land, it developed as a predator, sometimes chasing its prey, sometimes poised in patient ambush, creating an image of bait. Once fed, it returned to a gathering of its own kind, living in family groups much like present day whales.

With steely scales covering its snake like body it was well protected. It resided at the top of the food chain with no natural nemesis. The brain it had evolved almost telepathic capabilities, it communicated with its own with grunts and motions.

Although it could reduce its metabolism to near death, its mind remained active. How it longed to ply the seas again and note the changing of colors upon its own eyes. In the 1860's when men would fire torpedoes down the well shafts, it could feel the tremors and knew that one could free it or kill it, either way, the sweet joy of escape.

*****

Dwayne Smith was going to do it, he was determined. Although butterflies waged unholy battle in his stomach he approached her from behind. "Uh, hi Jessie," he almost stammered, "I was wondering if you had a date for the prom yet?"

Jessie caught her breath, Dwayne was the nicest, shyest, best looking boy in school and he was asking her to the prom! “Oh, I haven’t decided who I’ll go with. Who are you taking?”

“Uh, Jessie, I uh, I want to take you.” It took all he had to say that and not run away but he did manage to smile too.

“Me? You want to take me?” Dwayne’s heart took a trip down to his stomach. Jessie gave him an award winning smile and said, “Ok.”

Dwayne had it pretty rough growing up. His dad died when he was five, a scruffy drunk that whacked him more times than not. His mom remarried again to an overbearing man with little patience. Nothing Dwayne did was good enough, he became morose and withdrawn. The man’s lack of patience was his undoing though. He ran a stop sign riding his motorcycle and was killed by a Blue Bunny ice cream truck.

His next stepfather was different. His mother was actually laughing again. The man was polite and kind to Dwayne and now the poor kid was really mixed up. They did things as a family, going out to eat for no real reason, a trip to Conneaut to ride the Blue Streak, his mother screaming her head off as the cars went over the top. Dwayne kept his distance, waiting for the shoe to drop.

After almost a year the two of them went fishing. Dwayne’s mom begging off. She hated to bait the hook and handle the slippery fish. It was a crisp spring morning and they took up their positions about twenty feet apart, silently watching their bobbers.

“Dwayne,” the man said, “you don’t speak much. I respect that, it shows you think before you speak.”

Dwayne shrugged eyes straight ahead.

“Ah ha, now I got you communicating. That’s okay with me but in a year or so you’ll begin wanting to talk to girls and they will want to hear actual words.”

Dwayne just stood there shaking his head. He looked over at stepfather number two and said, "You don't know what it's like, you could be gone tomorrow."

"Well, that's true, but that's what makes any moment you spend happy so very special. The past is gone, but like scars on your hands the memories are always there. The future though, you can create your future however you wish."

Dwayne reeled in his line, checked his worm and cast it out again. Dwayne looked over at him and with his lower lip quivering said, "I want to be happy."

The man saw a tear start to fall and quickly looked out towards his bobber. "Why don't you run up to the truck and get us a couple pops?"

On the way back Dwayne saw his bobber go under and pull away. "Hey! I got something!" the pole began to slide towards the water. The man dropped his and ran over and dived for it, both of them sliding in the mud. The man stretched out and caught the handle just as it began to enter the river. Then they both had a grip on it sitting in the squishy mud.

"It's gotta be a monster!" yelled the stepfather. Twenty minutes later an eight pound big mouth was on the stringer. The men were wet, cold, and filthy, laughing like loony birds. Dwayne found the pops in the mud and washed his off in the river water, he turned to say something as he opened it and it sprayed right in the man's face. He grabbed his and returned the favor.

Dwayne's life changed that day. His grades improved dramatically, he spoke in full sentences, he laughed easily but he was still a little shy around other kids. Well, a lot shy, especially the girls. Jessie had always been nice to him however and really, she was the only girl he even thought about. Asking her to the prom their junior year was a very big step for him.

They really liked each other's company, spending time together at both houses over the summer. They got along very well, Bill found that the serious minded teenager had a talent for mechanics and he began to teach him some of the finer aspects of motors and trouble shooting. He even took him along as a helper on tow calls.

The young couple began their senior year with a passion. Dwayne had his driver's license but no car. Bill had a strict rule that nobody but Jessie drove her Jeep but when they went out of town, she insisted Dwayne drive. They never got caught. Bill was usually in the shop and if Woody saw them he never said. Jessie's mom was busy in Harrisburg now that she was a representative with her eye on a senate seat. Dwayne's mom and stepdad never interfered, although Dwayne did get an awkward lecture about condoms and such.

Jessie was captain of the cheerleader squad now and Dwayne tried out for the basketball team for the first time. He was an absolutely excellent athlete. He had been too shy to get out in front of a crowd before, being with Jessie changed everything. He found he loved the competition and played each game at full tilt.

The school won the division title and they advanced in the playoffs to the state final. The stands were packed with fans and proud parents, reporters, and college scouts. Both teams came to win and the action was fierce.

In the final period with South Forest up by five Dwayne got the ball at the top of the key and drove forward to the basket. As he jumped for his shot he was blocked from the side and he knocked heads with another player. He came down fast and hit his head again on the hardwood floor.

Out cold.

Silence in the gymnasium as the coach and trainer bent over him. His foot moved. He opened his eyes, in a couple minutes they helped him to his feet and led him to the locker room.

The fans cheered.

There was one minute and twenty seconds left on the clock. South Forest had one player left on the bench, Garth McFeaters. Garth had played some during the season after the game was a blowout; he had never had a chance to take a shot. He was in for Smith.

He missed both free throws, and half the fans let out a low groan. Holy Tree scored, intercepted a pass and scored again. Forty two seconds and the ball got away, Holy Tree recovering and scoring again.

Time out, South Forest.

Down by one, eleven seconds on the clock, Jessie was cheering her heart out with tears in her eyes. South Forest brought the ball in play, Holy Tree with a full court press, Garth ran for the corner. A pass ricocheted off a Holy Tree player right into the hands of McFeaters. He panicked and threw it towards the bucket; it bounced straight up and fell back through the hoop. The buzzer sounded, South Forest won their first state championship!

Pandemonium!

No one knew about the ambulance driving away from the back of the locker room.

Chapter Five

Dwayne was sitting in the locker room listening to the crowd roar. His head felt funny, a throbbing ache that felt dark and warm, and he couldn't focus his eyes. The trainer was holding a cold pack to the side of his head and an EMT was taking his vital signs, but it felt like he was far away, watching all this. He slipped into darkness.

They called the ambulance which was stationed nearby and he was rushed to Harrisburg Memorial. In less than an hour the decision was made to transfer him to Pittsburgh, and the flight was made. At the Allegheny General Trauma unit he was placed under the care of Doctor Rajid Humbarak, a neurological specialist. There was swelling on the brain and a possible lesion leaking blood. Dwayne came to once and said his head felt like it was splitting open, he then lapsed into a coma.

Forty four hours later there was no change, a slight fever occurred, but went away in a couple hours. His mom and stepdad were there as well as Jessie and her parents. The prognosis was not good, and surgery was discussed. The worried families exchanged small talk as Jessie stared out the window, her world having crumbled.

About three in the morning, Dwayne opened his eyes. He didn't know where he was, and felt a little scared. There were bright pinpoints of silver light floating in the air. He thought how pretty they looked with hints of scarlet neon behind them, and then slipped back into oblivion. The duty nurse came in to check on him about six. She was taking his pulse when his eyes opened, he tried to speak.

"No talking, you just take it easy. Can you understand me? Blink twice if you can." She was holding his hand, he knew her name was Sarah, she was feeling relief.

He blinked.

"I'm calling the doctor in, and I'm going to take your temperature, okay?" when she let go of his hand, he saw a reddish glow around her. He blinked again as he felt the thermometer slide into his mouth. He realized he couldn't move his head, what did that mean? He closed his eyes.

"Are you still with me?" he looked at her. "I'm going to give you a straw so you can take a sip of water, okay?" He blinked. "Good, very good, okay here you go. Good, that's all for now." Water had never been so satisfying.

A man wearing a white coat and another nurse walked in, the doctor touched him and Dwayne knew his name was Rajid, he was happy. He shone a light in each of his eyes and said, "Excellent, can you speak? Tell me your name."

"Dwayne, Dwayne Smith."

"Hello Dwayne I'm Dr. Humbarak, we have you immobilized on the bed, there is a nice padded clamp holding your head in place. Can you move your toes for me?"

The toes flexed twice.

"Good, now your fingers, right hand first please, okay, now left, excellent. The ladies here will take you for a CAT scan in a few minutes. How do you feel?"

"My head is too big."

"Ha, ha, yes. I'm sure it feels strange. I need you to stay awake until after the scan. Can you do that?"

Dwayne blinked and said, "I think so."

*****

Bill and Dwayne's stepdad were in the hospital cafeteria getting coffees for everyone. "Geez," Bill said, "he hit that floor hard, head first."

"Yeah," the other man said, "I heard a crack when he knocked heads with that other boy, that boy was hurting too. You know, Dwayne's a damn good kid, he and your daughter make a fine couple."

Bill paid for the drinks and said, "Thanks, I'm sure he'll be okay." There was a touch of trepidation in his voice.

The doctor had just arrived when they got back to the waiting area.

"Oh good, you are all here," he began, "I have good news, Dwayne is awake and alert." Jessie made a slight noise and leaned forward in her seat. "We are running tests right now that should take about an hour and then maybe one or two of you can see him."

Dwayne's stepdad spoke up. "Is he going to be okay?"

"We think so; he suffered two consecutive blows to the same area of the skull, which caused significant bruising to the bone. He has had a concussion and there may be bruising of the brain also. X-rays did not show any cracks in the skull. We will know more as we observe him. He is young, healthy and in excellent shape, prognosis is good."

The two mothers had been holding hands and now Jessie moved into her father's embrace. It was decided that Dwayne's mother and stepfather would see him first, then Jessie with her mom. When their turn came Patty begged off saying she'd just be in the way.

Jessie entered cautiously, and saw Dwayne laying there with that clamp still holding his head in place. She put on a brave smile as she approached and took his hand. When she touched him a flood of emotions bloomed in Dwayne's mind. He knew that everything she felt was as true and sincere as a human could feel. He knew she was his future.

"Hi," she began with a nervous smile, "you gotta quit all this laying around and get ready for school."

"Jessie, I..." he closed his eyes letting the feelings enfold him like a warm blanket on a cold night, "tell me, did we win the game?"

She gave a quick laugh of relief, "Yes, you jerk," and she told him all about Garth and the miracle bounce and how the trainer came running out during all the celebrating and told his mom about the ambulance, the ride to the hospital then the drive to Pittsburgh. After a bit the nurse looked in and told her she had to let him rest now. She gave him a gentle kiss on his lips and assured him she would be back.

The next morning he was feeling better and they had removed the clamp restricting his movement, raised the bed so he could sit up a little bit and eat breakfast. His mom and stepdad came in as soon as they could and were relieved to see him sitting up.

His mom put her hand over his and said, "Honey, we didn't want to tell you until after the game but there was a letter that morning stating that you have been accepted at Slippery Rock with a scholarship."

"It's a basketball scholarship however, you may have to give it up due to this injury," the man stated gravely, "but you're going to college regardless. Congratulations." His mom and her husband were grinning and beaming with pride.

Jessie meanwhile, had been waiting to see if Dwayne had been accepted anywhere before she made her decision of where she was going. Now it was definitely 'The Rock.' Bill and Patty left that day for home but Jessie stayed with Dwayne's parents until he was released three days later with strict orders to be very careful. He was still a little wobbly.

After a week the headaches faded and his balance was back so he returned to school. He endured all the wise cracks about hard heads and thick skulls with grace. The bell rang for seventh period and he took his desk at the back and opened his book for social studies. His pencil fell on the floor and rolled away. There was a scrap of paper laying there, it looked like a note that gets passed between friends during class and he touched it.

Becky McGill's face instantly filled his mind along with feelings of fear and shame that were very intense. He read the note, 'I know girls get pregs all the time but to their own dad?' the reply, from Sue Ann Harger read, 'What are you going to do?' That was all it said, he saw the whole thing in his mind, the drunken father, a frightened, crying Becky. He tore the note up and threw it away.

After school he told Jessie about it as she drove them home. She had to stop and pull over. "How can you possibly know who it was," she asked, "were their names on the note?"

"No, but I know it was her and Sue Ann as sure as I'm talking to you."

"That's ridiculous," she said with a roll of her eyes, "there is no way you could possibly know that. I'll keep an ear open. You know how fast rumors and bad news fly around."

But the rumor mill wasn't talking about things like that and in a couple days Jessie forgot all about it. Then on Monday came the shocking news that Becky McGill was dead. She had shot both her parents and then herself the night before. Sue Ann Harger broke down in tears when she heard the news in homeroom that morning. By noon the whole school had learned the awful circumstances of Becky's home life, the drunken incestuous father, the uncaring mother, the pregnancy.

Jessie waited until she and Dwayne were alone in the Jeep headed home. "Wow, you really called the shot on that one."

Dwayne shook his head, "I feel so bad, like, maybe I could have said something to somebody and got her some help somehow."

"Dwayne, if I didn't believe you at first then nobody would have and Becky would have denied it 'til the day she died. Oh, that didn't come out right, what am I saying?"

"Somehow, I can touch someone, something they had handled, even doorknobs tell me things. I have no clue how this started but I couldn't do it before the accident. It's very distracting."

"Do you want to see a doctor about this? Wait, I read about a woman who said she could do that very thing in some paranormal book. She helped the police find missing persons."

"No, no doctors," Dwayne made a stopping motion with his hands, "they'll just put me in some crazy place and I'll never see you again. No, we just won't tell anybody."

Jessie nodded her head and pulled into Dwayne's driveway. "Okay, we'll keep this between us. I will never tell a soul even if we break up."

"We will be together for a long, long time. I'm sure of that." Dwayne smiled at her as he got out then leaned back in to kiss her, "A very, very, long time."

Graduation day came and went. They had a party at Jessie's house with the parents and some friends like Mary Bowser and her family. There were watches given and necklaces exchanged, talk of college or jobs. Dwayne's buddy Garth was signing up for the Air Force. He told Dwayne he could make as much as a pilot fixing airplanes, without ever having to take a chance of falling out of the sky.

Patty stood up at about the midway point and announced her upcoming bid for a state senate seat. That's the way she was, things always had to be about her, Jessie thought as she rolled her eyes and looked apologetically at all her friends. Bill stood up clapping and said to everybody present, "There's beer and soft drinks outside in the tub, but if any of you graduates want to drink there will be no driving. I'm gonna have a Straubs or two myself, come on let's get out of this stuffy room."

Grandma Laverne came over to Jessie and took her hand, "I'm so proud of you," she beamed, "and that young man you seem infatuated with is certainly handsome enough."

"Thanks Grammy," Jessie smiled, "he's the man for me."

"Well," Laverne laughed, "there's plenty of time for that. Now plan on being alone with me tomorrow, there's a few things I need to talk to you about."

"Sure, but if it's about boys I already had that little talk a long time ago."

"Oh my goodness no," Laverne laughed out loud, "no, it's about the future, your future."

"Oh, okay, I'll see you in the morning, before noon."

"Good, now you go enjoy yourself, you only graduate high school once." Laverne watched her walk away and smiled.

Jessie walked outside with the other people and saw her mom talking with Dwayne. She had her hand on his arm, like she was holding him from running away.

"... and another thing, there will be no hints of scandal coming from that damn college either." Jessie overheard as she approached. "Mother! What in the world?" Dwayne backed away, he looked like he was gonna be sick.

"Oh nothing," Patty snipped, "I was simply informing your boyfriend here that I will not tolerate you being dragged into any trouble while at college, it would hurt my career."

"Well, we haven't done anything to be ashamed of yet, and I'm quite sure we won't." Jessie was getting angry, "Maybe you've had enough to drink already, please don't spoil this night for me."

"Just don't spoil your whole damn life, and embarrass me." Patty turned and walked away.

"Dwayne, you okay? You don't look so good." Dwayne had seen enough through Patty's touch to realize he didn't want to know much more about the aspiring senator. He looked at Jessie with a stricken grimace on his face.

"Dwayne?"

"There's something wrong with your mother."

"Yeah, she's a self- centered bitch, and cares nothing for no one but herself."

"No, it's, it's like she's dead inside or something. I can't describe it."

"Forget it, she's a politician. Come on, I want one of those beers. Dad hardly ever drinks one; Woody must be on duty tonight."

The next morning Jessie got up and found Laverne at the table waiting on her. "You want some coffee?" Laverne asked, "You were up a lot later than me."

"No, I want some juice though," and poured herself a glass.

"Say, where's that young man of yours?" Laverne asked, her face a mask of innocence.

"He went home, Mom really freaked him out. She can be such a bitch." Jessie empathized as she sat down.

"Yes, she believes herself to be very important." Laverne said as she stared at her cup. Then she looked up at Jessie and smiled, "She left a couple hours ago, now miss college girl tell me which courses of study you wish to pursue."

"I'm interested in biology and anthropology," Jessie said with a clear, even tone then added, "of course I'm interested in a lot of things."

"Good, those are fine subjects to major in. However, in the future you will need some other skills as well. You will inherit the fruits of my 'hobby', as Buddy used to call it. I want you to take courses in accounting, geology and real estate if you think you can handle it."

Jessie had both hands around her juice glass and she nodded, "But why all that? It's just a couple camp lots or so, right?"

Laverne chuckled. "That's exactly what Buddy thought also. My 'hobby' is paying for your education." She let that sink in a wee bit. "It's my gift to you and your father; he's been a fine, steady man."

"Grandma, that's a LOT of money," Jessie exclaimed, "I thought Mom and Dad..."

Laverne flicked her fingers at an imaginary bug, "It's a gift nonetheless, your father works hard but he doesn't make a fortune, your mother contributes nothing." She glanced down, "We could call it an investment, I think you're worth it."

"Oh Grammy, thank you so much, I'll do my best to make you proud."

"You always have sweetheart. Now today, you can make me proud by helping with your father's books."

Jessie rolled her eyes.

*****

Patty was pounding down I-80 in her Mercedes coupe. She was thinking with a scowl on her face. 'That damned kid's gonna get drunk. Then get her butt arrested at that damned college. Probably gonna get herself knocked up too. Can't have that. Bill thinks she'll be fine, idiot. He let her drink last night, her and that scared little boy. She's probably pregnant already.' She hit the steering wheel with the palm of her hand. 'I don't need SCANDAL!'

She took the exit for Bellefonte and headed south. She stopped at McDonalds and used the restroom, then got a small coffee to go. She noticed a payphone on her way out and paused. She dug around in her purse and found a number, she punched in the numbers.

"Senator Cornet's office, how may I help you?"

"Yes, this Forest County Representative Patricia Lyons, would you tell the senator I will accept his offer for lunch and he may call my office to arrange a date and time. Thank you."

Dougie Cornet was a handsome man, married though. She knew the party was grooming him for the governor's office. It wouldn't hurt to be friendly. His secretary knocked and walked into his office.

"I have a message from Patricia Lyons." She bent over to place it on his desk. He looked at her cleavage. "Do you want anything else?"

He smiled, "You could lock the door for a little while."

She smiled.

*****

Dwayne was informed by his doctor that he should avoid all contact sports that could possibly lead to another head injury. He talked with the coach at Slippery Rock and it was decided that his playing basketball was too risky.

He lost his scholarship. He told his mother. His stepfather took him to the bank to apply for a student loan. They had to wait a few days for approval.

Jessie told her grandmother all about it. Laverne simply said, "I see." The next day she paid a visit to the bank. The loan was approved.

The young couple discovered that college was much harder than high school. They supported each other though and stayed away from the party scene. Not to say they didn't have any fun, they did of course, only moderately. Dwayne wanted to teach American history and Jessie elected anthropology as her major. Dwayne learned that to keep his sanity intact, he must avoid touching other people and objects he didn't have to, or to wear gloves when practical.

The four years passed quickly. Patty was elected to the state senate and Bill took on more accounts, hiring two more mechanics. Laverne continued to dabble in her hobby.

Their senior year found them sharing a one bedroom rental at Rock Falls Park. Six weeks before graduation she couldn't wait any longer. Jessie informed her soul mate that she was definitely pregnant. Dwayne sat there, their future looked good, both of them would have their degrees soon and he was completing his student teaching requirement at Moniteau High School. A baby changed everything.

"Now, you're pregnant now?" Dwayne was incredulous.

Jessie nodded her head, "Well, what did you expect, these things happen." She reached over and touched his hand. He was pensive for a moment then a smile lit up his face.

'I'm gonna be somebody's daddy, oh Jessie this is fantastic!"

Chapter Six

In a cheap motel outside Harrisburg, Patty was telling the lieutenant governor how good he was. Dougie Cornet was lapping it up. They had been seeing each other at this same motel every other week or so for three years now. She hadn't been that hard of a contest, he knew she was ambitious and he could push the right buttons. They were playing each other's tune.

"So tell me Doug," Patty ran her hand across his chest, "you have someone in mind for a running mate?"

"Nothing definite yet but I am thinking of a woman." He was grinning at her, she smiled.

The next day Patty was in the hallway of the senate building when she saw Dougie with two men she had never seen before. Doug saw her coming and held up his hand, halting the conversation.

"Ah Senator," he said as he took her proffered hand in both of his, "we were just discussing Forest County."

"I hope you weren't talking about our lack of traffic lights." She gave a quick laugh and nodded at the men, "Gentlemen," she greeted them with her winning smile.

"Allow me to introduce Mr. Richardson and Mr. Hunt of Dallas, Texas," Doug smiled.

"Dallas, oil men I presume?" She gave them an inquiring look.

Mr. Hunt cleared his throat, "Yes that is correct. We were discussing mineral rights with Mr. Cornet."

"Oh I see, well gentlemen we could certainly use some good jobs in Forest County, excuse me but I have a meeting, ta ta." She turned and the men watched her wiggle away.

Richardson looked at Cornet inquisitively. "Don't worry," Dougie smiled, "I can guarantee she will do as I say."

"Excellent, this will be a major investment, we don't like complications." Mr. Hunt asserted.

One year prior the geologists employed by the oil company confirmed a natural gas deposit larger than any other previously discovered deep below western Pennsylvania in what was known as the Marcellus Shale Deposit. Techniques still being developed by drillers were proving up and they believed they could, in a short time, be able to reach it and exploit it.

This information was being kept confidential. Dougie was assured of full financial support in his run for governor for some minor concessions to the oil men. They were very interested in the Forest/Venango County area, especially in the old Pithole grounds. Within a few months depleted oil leases were bought up and if possible the land also.

This was accomplished with no fanfare or public knowledge. The folks approached by these men were surprised and most thought the offers a stroke of good luck. A few, like Jessie's grandmother were suspicious. She refused to sign, at least until she had more information. She discreetly made inquiries.

The pregnant couple quietly graduated college and just as quietly were married by a justice of the peace. They moved in with Bill who was pretty much living by himself, along with Laverne. Duane put applications in at the local schools and worked in the garage with Bill and the crew while he waited for a call. Jessie spent her time with her granny, now long retired from the courthouse.

During their many conversations while they cooked, crocheted, cleaned, and kept busy Laverne told her granddaughter about the 'speculators' and how she had acquired not only the old Yoder place, (now a ruin), but the old Holmren farm that abutted the Pithole State Historical site. She told Jessie that just by the interest those men had, the value of the property increased and there must be a reason they wanted it. She said she would never sell until she learned the truth.

Four days later, on the morning of her seventy third birthday, she was watching kittens play when suddenly, she died. Patty was aghast. She had arrived home from the capitol the night before, as she had a party planned for her mother that evening with thirty important guests. She got on the phone. Bill had to use the shop line to call the ambulance and the funeral home. Dwayne held Jessie as she cried.

One of the calls Patty made was to Doug Cornet's answering service informing him of this latest development and how this uncomplicated the issue they had been discussing. Dougie smiled, his life just got a little easier.

That evening, as the bereaved family sat at dinner Patty showed her irritation. "All those phone calls, and every one of them wanted to know details, I hate to tell the same story over and over again. This has really been embarrassing, she couldn't have picked a better day to die, nooo, not my mother. That party was well planned." Patty snorted in disgust.

"Patty," Bill began but she cut him off short.

"You don't say a word, you better hope she didn't leave this place to some damned church or something. This is all you got." Bill stared at her.

"Mom," Jessie said, "she left it to Dad."

"Really, I suppose you had something to do with that, and how do you know all her business all of a sudden? You do know she was going to sell me the property along Pithole road don't you?"

"I don't think so Mother, we had just talked about that property a few days ago. Can't you just give it a rest? Grammy just died, and all you're concerned about is that stupid party you had planned that she didn't want." Jessie's voice was quivering.

"Doesn't matter, I was her daughter and I'm sure she left everything to me and that air headed sister of mine." Patty said with a toss of her head.

"Enough," said Bill, "let's let the poor woman rest in peace." Patty stormed off upstairs.

Four days later the funeral was drawing to a close. Patty had given a splendid performance as the grieved daughter for all the viewer's and reporters. Now, at the graveside a thunder storm broke as the preacher said the final words and everyone ran for cover. One figure, dressed all in black as fitted the occasion remained by the graveside. He was seen to grin as he kicked some muddy gravel in the hole. It made hollow thunks as it landed on the casket. The funeral party was served lunch and drinks at the fire hall and as these affairs go, was wound down early.

They were sitting around the table later having coffee when the phone rang, "I'll get it," said Bill and took it in the living room. Patty was showing aggravation as she sat there, her legs crossed and her foot bouncing as she assaulted her Parliament. She was upset she had to wait another day for the will reading. Jessie and Dwayne remained silent.

"That was Ollie White, he said the judge is postponing the reading as there is some complication with the property and he wants to be sure everything is in order." Bill said as re-entered the kitchen.

"How long?" Patty said rolling her eyes.

"He wasn't sure, about two weeks he thinks." Bill shrugged.

"Great, okay, I'm going back to Harrisburg," Patty snubbed out her butt on the saucer and got up. She turned to Bill, "Don't be going through any of her stuff while I'm gone," she looked at Jessie and Dwayne, "you two either, I don't want anything to mysteriously disappear."

"Bitch," Jessie said after she clomped up the stairs. Bill made a shushing motion with his hand, "Don't," was all he said. A few minutes later she came down with her suitcase, they heard from the door, "Make sure that damn lawyer calls my office!" the door slammed and then the car started.

Bill sat down and Jessie got him a fresh cup, "I don't understand why she said, 'everything you have'."

"Forget it Dad, she is so out of touch. Grammy told me you would never have to worry." Jessie worried at a slice of cake picking it apart with her fork.

"Apparently your Mom is taking this whole thing pretty hard, I'm sure she'll calm down soon you know how she gets. She should have been an actress." Bill said this and grinned.

"Dad I..." the phone rang. Bill took it off the kitchen wall, "This is Pennsylvania State Police dispatch. We need two wreckers at the intersection of Poland Hill road and Route 62. Be advised that one vehicle is a semi- truck and trailer." Bill looked at Dwayne who nodded and said, "No problem, on my way."

Bill fired up his Marmon semi-wrecker and Dwayne got in the Chevy flatbed. Jessie spoke with Dwayne a moment then climbed in with Bill. "Dad, we need to talk about Grandma."

"Jesus Jessie, we're on a call, is this important?" Bill put the truck in gear and headed out the drive.

"I don't think Mom is going to be too happy at the will reading. Grammy told me what she was going to do."

Bill was shifting gears, gaining speed, the Chevy right behind him. "What the heck are you talking about?"

"She said the house and the business with the ten acres are yours, period. Mom isn't getting anything."

"Nothing, she will explode. Who is she leaving everything else to?"

Jessie looked at him and in a small voice said, "Me."

Bill looked at her and sighed. The police lights were visible now and Bill turned on his caution flashers and top rollers. He slowed at the first car and the officer waved him on. The semi was still on the road and the berm, upright and only slightly cock eyed. Underneath the trailer slammed up on the trailer wheels was what had been a car.

The police had finished putting out flares and were directing the light traffic around the wreck. Bill saw there were at least five cruisers and two ambulances still at the scene and told Jessie to stay in the truck. Bill got out as

Office Brown came up to the truck, "Hi Bill, looks like one of the worst, multiple deaths, young girls, bad situation."

The semi had been headed north and was gaining speed for the hill ahead. Four teenage girls had ran a stop sign and pulled right in front of the truck. The semi- tractor climbed right over the compact car crushing it. The sliding locked up trailer wheels pushed it ahead trapping it underneath the trailer. Bill saw the truck driver sitting in the back of a cruiser, he was crying.

The girls had been cruising around the back roads drinking a couple wine coolers, smoking a little pot, listening to music and jabbering away like any group of young ladies would do. Nobody was worried at that point why, they had ran the stop sign.

Bill assessed the situation and backed his wrecker up to the front of the Frieghtliner. Both front tires were flat and the bumper bent back into them, oil was leaking from the motor. He had Dwayne get into position and hook on to the car. Dwayne came out from under the trailer and had to puke, "The smell," he told Officer Bells who was standing there.

Bill placed his "J" hooks under the front end and raised the tires off the ground. He then ran jumper air lines back to the trailer and told Dwayne to get ready. He backed the big rig up enough for Dwayne to winch the wrecked car out from underneath, then the EMTs, firemen and coroner took over.

It was bad. Four young, vibrant girls had been crushed to death. They used their new "jaws of life" tool to remove the roof. The Coroner and EMTs did their best to separate the bodies. It was three hours before the police told Bill to go ahead and put the car in impound. Jessie was sure it was Chancey Wainwright's car as she saw the fox painted on the fender. She was the preacher's daughter at the Lutheran Church. She had always been a little wild.

Bill was sweating and panting when he came over to inspect the car on the flatbed. "Okay," he said, "take it home and we want to put it in the third bay, it's impounded." Dwayne nodded and got in the cab. Bill caught Jessie's arm, "Ride with me Honey." She shrugged at Dwayne and walked with her dad.

"You ok?" she asked, "you look like you just ran a race."

"Yeah, yeah, it's just been a long day and those poor kids..." he climbed in the driver's seat and they started pulling the long heavy load. About halfway home he asked, "What're yinz gonna name the baby?"

"Oh, uh, if it's a girl then either Celeste or Starla and a boy will be named William Albinious after you and Dwayne's stepdad.

"Huh, Starla's nice I like that, but William Albinious? His initials will be w, a, s, was? No, Albinious William would be better." He looked at her and smiled. She grinned and shook her head.

He pulled into the parking lot and stopped. "Go open the gate, then turn on the lights and open up the third bay for Dwayne. I'll drop this and be right in."

"Okay," she said and climbed out of the truck. Dwayne pulled in at this point and saw the trailer disappear around back. The lights came on and soon the door was rising. He maneuvered around and backed it in. Jessie gave him a little help and soon the demolished car was slid off the flatbed and flat on the floor. They were both looking at it as they waited on Bill to give everything a final check. Jessie got her camera and took some pictures.

"This has certainly been a long day," Jessie said as she fussed with her focus. "It seems like the funeral was last week not this morning."

"Yeah, a lot happened for sure." Dwayne was looking out the door he was getting a little anxious. "Let me go see what's keeping Bill, he should have been here by now." Jessie walked with him.

They walked through the shadows to the back lot, and when they saw him lying on the ground they broke into a run. He was laying on his side his clipboard a couple feet away. Dwayne knelt by his side and examined him, "He's still breathing but he's unconscious," he said to Jessie, "Stay with him, I'll go call 911." He leapt up and took off running. Jessie knelt in his place and took Bill's hand, it was cold.

"Oh Daddy, please wake up," she touched his forehead and stroked his hair, tears running freely down her face. Dwayne came running back.

"They're on the way," he said, "how's he doing?"

"He's sooo cold, but his hand jerked a little," Jessie looked up at her husband, a sad frown on her face.

Dwayne looked around. Bill was about twenty feet from the truck. It had been disconnected and shut off. He had been on his way to the shop. He had simply collapsed for some reason. He reached down and touched Bill's hand. He saw a grinning snake's head on a man's body and it struck towards him. The ambulance pulled in.

Chapter Seven

"I'm telling you what I saw," Mike Fine the truck driver said to the policeman sitting across the table from him, "there was a man running alongside that car, and there was no way I didn't hit him."

Officer Bells shook his head, "Look Mr. Fine, we found no other bodies under the truck or on the road or off the side. I think we're going to have you taken to the hospital and check your blood and urine for alcohol and drugs."

"Go ahead, I lead a good Christian life and just started my work week. You'll find nothing, just like you say you found at the wreck." The driver answered assuredly. "Hell, the way those poor kids were mangled, there could have been another body in there and you wouldn't know it."

Officer Bells sighed, "Come on, we're taking a ride."

*****

Bill had a stroke. He was taken to Allegheny Mercy in Pittsburgh where he was placed in intensive care. They called but couldn't locate Patty, they kept trying.

"She probably got tired and checked into a motel on the way back to Harrisburg." Dwayne said as he handed Jessie a cup of coffee in the waiting room. They were both exhausted after closing up the business, driving to Titusville only to find out they had to drive to Pittsburgh and then making that trip.

The doctor came in and told them Bill was in stable condition but the extent of the stroke was unknown at this time. He advised them to get some rest it was 5:43am. They got a room nearby, called and told the hospital where they were. Dwayne called his parents and woke them up. He told them what had happened and asked his mom to keep trying to get through to Patty. They kicked their shoes off, lay down on the bed and were soon sound asleep.

Albinious finally reached Patty's secretary at 8:45am, she swore she would inform the senator of the emergency as soon as she walked in. at that moment Patty was in her car on the way to her office and still pissed at her dead mother.

How dare she not have left everything to me, I am the most successful one of the entire family. Her sister Tina had been featured in art magazines and in several gallery exhibits, but Patty was sure it was her fame as a senator that made her sister so noticed. She might get something, but in wouldn't be much. She chuckled at that thought, her older sister, little miss clueless would be overjoyed if the old bat had left her a dust mop.

Her damn mother, dying on her birthday, couldn't have waited until the party was over, noooo, I had to make all those embarrassing phone calls to cancel the party and each and every one of those assholes had to hear all the details. During the party would have been the best. Now that would have been dramatic!

She had been exhausted, the night before when she had finally reached her condo; she unplugged her phones and went to bed frustrated. She thought about the day Dougie had asked her about the Pithole property. He told her there were some very wealthy people interested in it and records had shown that her mother currently owned it.

He explained about the impending boom that would happen with the gas industry and how important and profitable it would be to be in on the ground floor. He had her hooked when he told her about the royalties and lease payments that would be hers for the rest of her life. It was, in his words an "Assured fortune." All she had to do is control that property. She would even garner praise as bringing jobs into her district. It was a good political move.

She entered her office at two minutes to nine and her secretary, Gladis Damato, gave her the urgent message. She closed her door and went over to her antique cherry desk, once owned by Andrew Carnegie. There were several messages laid out in chronological order. She rearranged them in order of importance as she called the familiar number she held in her hand.

Albinious answered on the second ring. "Patty, thank God," he said, "we've been trying to reach you all night. Bill had a stroke; he's in Pittsburgh at Allegheny Mercy. They got him in intensive care."

"A stroke, Oh no, poor Billy," she still loved her husband in her way. He ran the business, took care of their home and on occasion they made safe, friendly love. The exciting sex she had with Dougie was more self- centered and had little to do with affection. "Climbing the ladder" is what she told herself but the whole affair was like a cheaply made porn movie. That didn't matter as the golden rung was now clearly in sight.

Albinious got her caught up on the tragic accident and the aftermath. "Patty now listen, it doesn't look good for Bill. He hasn't regained consciousness yet but is breathing on his own. You need to get there as soon as you can."

"I will, thank you for calling." She hung up. A thousand thoughts ran through her mind, things were happening a little too quickly. She pushed the intercom button. "Gladis, cancel everything for today and tomorrow and get me a flight to Pittsburgh. My husband had a stroke."

Woody showed up at work about seven. He had his own keys to the place and let himself in to punch the time clock. Bill's clipboard was on the counter and after he opened up and made coffee he read the towing bill. Curious, he went to the third bay's man door. He unlocked it and turned on the light. He dropped his coffee, it splashed on his leg but he didn't feel it. A man all dressed in black wearing a wide brimmed hat stood on the opposite side of the wrecked car.

"Who the fleck'r you," Woody roared?

The man tilted his head back and laughed, he then vanished. The creature was pleased as it rested in its ancient enclosure. It had fed well the night before on the four life energies its avatar had absorbed at the wreck. The terror the girls were feeling at the time of their deaths had heightened the force of the energies. Running beside the speeding Subaru and banging on the roof all the way down Poland Hill road while the girls were screaming had been stimulating. Later that night, scaring the shit out of the tow truck driver as he was working had been icing on the cake. It was having some real fun.

Woody was shaken, he had never saw a ghost before and wasn't sure he had now. He quickly shut and locked the door, leaving the lights on. He thought about shutting them off, looked at the door and decided no flecken way. By that time Jake and Roy showed up and the phone was ringing.

It was Albinious, as Woody listened he realized he'd be running things for a while. He assured Biney that he could handle things and to tell the family not to worry about the business, "They got more than enough to worry about right now."

He hung up and stared at the phone for a long second. He looked up and saw Roy and Jake staring at him. "Bill had a stroke; they flew him down to Pittsburgh. It doesn't look good. We will keep the business running, Roy, your boy still looking for a part time job?" Roy nodded. "Good, call him in and both of you stay the hell away from the third bay. There's a quarantined impound in there, the door stays locked." He shuddered as he turned towards the office.

When Patty's plane was approaching Pittsburgh, Jessie and Dwayne were having coffee and getting ready to return to the hospital. "I'll call my stepdad when we get over there and see if he got hold of your mother yet," he told her. She looked up at him with baleful eyes and nodded.

"It's just that such an awful lot has happened in such a short amount of time," she said as she moved her spoon around. "First Grandma on her birthday, the funeral, dealing with Mother, those poor girls and now poor Dad," tears made their first appearance.

Dwayne caught a falling teardrop with his thumb, he hadn't told her yet of what he had seen when he touched her father. It could keep. He looked at her for a minute and then finished his cup, "Come on, it's time we got over there." Jessie fixed her face, and then they walked to the hospital and the dreaded waiting room.

Patty climbed out of the private Cessna and walked into the airport. She spied a bank of payphones and made a bee line. "Hello? Dougie, yes, it's me. Listen, I'm in Pittsburgh, Bill had a stroke and I don't know how long I'll be here..." she then told him of the delay in her impending inheritance and what that could mean. She said her goodbyes and made her way out to the front and took a cab.

She walked in the waiting room to find the doctor talking to Jessie and Dwayne. "Oh Mom, you made it, I'm so glad you're here," Jessie stood and hugged her.

The doctor cleared his throat and said, "You must be Senator Lyons, please allow me to bring you up to date on your husband's condition."

Jessie took her mother's hand. He explained in general terms just what a stroke was and informed them that it had been a massive one. He was not confidant that Bill would recover and if he did, he would be greatly diminished. He allowed the wife and daughter to see him.

Dwayne remained in the waiting room. As he lingered he picked up a magazine and thumbed through it. One article caught his eye. He read that massive amounts of natural gas had been discovered in a deep shale deposit stretching from New York to Kentucky, centered in Pennsylvania. The article went on to explain that new drilling techniques had been developed to reach and exploit this ancient bonanza. The monetary value was in the billions. He made a mental note to show this to Jessie.

Patty and Jessie returned, Jessie was crying and Dwayne stood to take her in his arms. "He died, Dwayne," said Patty as she looked out the window, "we were holding his hands and the machines made an awful sound. Then the medical people pushed us out of the way, like we didn't matter." Jessie sobbed harder.

The next few days were a jumble of images and emotions for Jessie. Patty had a small entourage of aides show up to take care of arrangements. Woody closed the shop for the funeral, only keeping the wrecker lines open and handled all the calls.

Two hundred people attended the funeral. Patty played the bereaved widow beautifully to the press and cameras. The Lieutenant Governor arrived and stood stoically by her side, the photograph made front pages all over the state.

Jessie's knees buckled as the casket was lowered in the ground, Dwayne gave her support as she sobbed. Finally the amens were said and the crowd strolled away.

Attorney Oliver White called the next day. Judge Bannet decided to save time and read Mrs. Tater's and Mr. Lyon's wills at the same time and had set the date for the following Wednesday. Patty decided to return to the capitol. All during the funeral activities she had been on the phone as much as possible. She made another call and had a rental delivered.

When it came she stood and said to Jessie and Dwayne, "I'll be back Tuesday night, and I hope I can get some work done before someone else dies." She gave a toss of her head and slammed the door.

Jessie had been watching with her mouth open, "Well goodbye, love you too," she said to the back of the door, "God, it's like everything was just a waste of time for her."

"Forget her for now Jess," Dwayne got up and stretched, "we got a lot of work to catch up on. Let's go see Woody."

The next morning Jessie and Dwayne rose early. Jessie tackled the books in the office and sorted through the invoices as Dwayne helped Woody reopen the shop and get things caught up.

About ten thirty, on the morning that Bill died, Detective David Sike and Trooper Bells arrived to inspect the wrecked car in bay three. They said their condolences and got to work. Before they entered the room they put a little Vicks under their noses to mask the smell. Woody came over and unlocked the door. The policemen entered and shut the man door but opened the big bay door to let in the fresh air. Nobody noticed that the lights were still on but Woody. They began their methodical examination.

They found two purses which they bagged and tagged, both were crusted with dried blood and body fluids. There were a couple empty wine cooler bottles and a camera. They would develop the film and see if there were any photos of the girls drinking the beverages. They took many photographs of their own and made copious notes. They called Woody over and told him they were rescinding the impound order but cautioned him to place a tarp over the wreck until the insurance companies had a look at it.

As they were leaving, Detective Sike noticed Jessie's Jeep and remembered the one case he hadn't solved.

Chapter Eight

Patty called Dougie at his residence as soon as she got back to her condominium. An unfamiliar voice answered and Patty informed her that Senator Lyons was calling for the Lieutenant Governor.

"Oh yes, Senator Lyons... Forest County, I'm Douglas's wife, Madeline, we met last spring at the Children's Hospital fund raiser. I heard about your tragedies, I'm so sorry."

"Madeline. How wonderful to hear your voice again. Thank you for your concern. I hope I'm not interrupting anything."

"No, nothing important, here he is now. Let's get together sometime."

"Yes, sure, lunch perhaps?"

Dougie got on the line. She told him about the wills being read the next week. He told her that deals had been made and money was waiting to be exchanged. It was all waiting on the property owner's signature. She assured him that as soon as the property was under her control they could move forward. He told her that new projections were showing a billion dollar enterprise was expected and it all hinged on the first exploratory well they wanted to sink on the Pithole land.

Patty hung up the phone and fantasized about the power that much money would bring to her. She would not let anything stand in her way. She would be generous and give her daughter the garage business and the house. She smiled to herself, that act would enhance her public image. It embarrassed her to speak of her humble beginnings, now it would simply be an amusing anecdote. After that she would begin to find a new husband worthy of her ambitions. Dougie will just have to get a divorce. She couldn't wait until next Wednesday.

Jessie came out of the obstetrician's office with a smile. The baby, now well into its second trimester, was healthy and developing normally. She had been worried that all the emotions she had just gone through would harm the fetus.

She had called her dad's tax consultant and they both examined the shop books. They were found to be detailed and in perfect order. Bill had always maintained that for a business to be truly successful you had to be totally honest in all aspects.

As she poked around in the desk drawers she found a photo of her mom and dad at the old place. They looked so young and happy, him with his arm around her. She got a frame for it and hung in on the office wall. She smiled as she looked at it, wondering what they had been thinking at that moment.

Dwayne came in and opened the small fridge and rustled around for lunch, "Not much in here, we got any bologna up at the house?"

"Oh there might be something like that. I'll go take a look. Why don't you come up too, I'll make some soup also."

On Tuesday Patty and Dougie managed a two hour tryst. He reiterated again the importance of her coming inheritance and what it would mean to both of them. She told him that she was a free woman now and that she was thinking of remarrying again, insinuating that he would be her choice.

Dougie replied that he couldn't possibly divorce Madeline now so close to his bid for governor, "No, she would have to have an accident or something." He said that with a look of perplexity on his face that did not escape her notice. She didn't say a word.

Jessie and Dwayne were watching TV when Patty walked in at nine that night. "I'm exhausted and I need a drink," she said as she plunked her suitcase down beside the couch, "maybe my son in law could make himself useful and run that up to my room for me, thank you."

Jessie got up and went to the cabinet to see what they had, "Uh, there's some gin and I know we have some ginger ale. Will that be alright?"

"Yes, fine, anything," Patty said waving her hand around as she lit a cigarette. She plopped down into the overstuffed chair, "I need an ashtray too, damn it. Why don't you have any out, you knew I was coming." She crossed her legs, her foot started moving up and down.

"You okay," asked Dwayne as he reentered the room, "you look upset." Jessie came in and handed her the drink mixed in a tall glass with a yellow daisy painted on it.

Patty looked at it, "Two ice cubes," she groused.

"Sorry, that's all we had, I refilled the tray," Jessie shrugged and sat back down.

"Well, it certainly keeps in sync with my perfect day. It rained the whole way here, the trucks on the interstate were horrible, I have pressing issues in the capitol, and I have no idea how long all this 'will' business will take. Upset? You have no clue."

"Mom, relax you're home now," Jessie said, "you're safe and you can rest."

"Home… it's not mine anymore. I may have grown up in this shit hole but it's not my home. You can have it with my blessings." Patty finished off her drink, "Get me another one. I don't care about the ice."

Dwayne took the glass and headed in to the kitchen.

"Mom, Aunt Tina called. She was summoned to the will reading also."

"Wonderful," Patty said the word dripping with sarcasm, "the slices get smaller. Have you gone through your father's things yet?"

"Not upstairs, that's your room too. The office yes, there's a real nice picture of you and him out there and…"

"I'll get what I want out of here tomorrow. Do what you will with everything else." She grabbed the glass out of Dwayne's hand and headed up the stairs.

Dwayne looked at Jessie who shook her head, "Maybe she'll feel better in the morning, all this traveling and who knows what she has to put up with in

Harrisburg. No wonder she's cranky." Dwayne looked up the stairs and shook his head. "This hasn't been too easy on you either."

Patty was searching in the closet, finally locating the handgun Bill had found all those years ago, she slipped it in her suitcase. She could still smell Bill in the bed and she thought how sad it was he had been content with his little empire as she drifted off to sleep.

She awoke the next morning and found the house to herself as she made her way to the kitchen. Jessie had left a fresh pot of coffee on for her. She poured a cup and sat at her accustomed place at the table. She lit a cigarette and noticed the kid had put an ashtray out for her as well, she sighed.

She was thinking she needed to call her secretary when she looked out through the sliding glass doors into the backyard. She gave a little jump. A man was standing just inside the wood line. A man dressed all in black. He gave a huge grin as their gazes met and he stared, straight back at her then vanished. She had seen that man before, she was sure of it, but where? She wondered if there might be something wrong with her.

Jessie came in the front, "Morning Mom, oh my, you okay? You look like you saw a ghost!"

"I..." she spilled her coffee, "I, uh, I'm just nervous that's all. There's a lot riding on what your grandmother put in her will."

Jessie grabbed a couple paper towels, "Grammy knew what she was doing, I'm sure she thought out everything."

"My daughter Jessie Jayne, always so practical," Patty replied, with a glance out the back that Jessie didn't notice.

The ladies dressed and got ready to go, riding together in Jessie's Jeep.

---- --- ----

In the early summer of 1646, a French Jesuit priest and two Mohawk guides paddled down the Allegheny River. The priest, Jacques Rochard, was bringing the word of God into the virgin land. Tall for his time at six feet and one inch, he wore the black clothing of his order.

To the natives, black was the color of peace and he was not feared; besides he came alone. He found he could learn the sign language with ease and began to pick up enough words and phrases to be understood to the various tribes. He was on his way to the Seneca Nation along the Allegheny.

They stopped early that day at the mouth of a small creek and set off hunting. They wanted to bring fresh meat as a gift to the Seneca. They found a set of very large bear tracks and decided that would be a perfect gift, it would give them respect and prestige.

They followed the tracks for about three miles when suddenly the brave in the lead stopped. There was a huge black snake in his path. He noticed more snakes on both sides; all the men saw black snakes. They were surrounded. Then snakes dropped from the trees above them, hundreds of them, they were overwhelmed.

They didn't kill the priest right away the creature manifesting the black snakes had never seen a white man before. It studied the man who was on his knees with both hands clasp before him moving his lips. It decided to use that model for its man avatar. The man stopped what he was doing and the snakes swarmed over, smothering him.

---- --- ----

Patty and Jessie were ten minutes early at the courthouse. They found Patty's sister, Tina, with her three grown sons seated outside the courtroom. They greeted each other cordially. Ollie White, Esquire and Joe Fontana, Tina's attorney, turned the corner and strode down the hall.

Ollie hated will readings. There were either embarrassing tears or shouting matches. Sometimes things went well. He knew Senator Lyons however, he was apprehensive. They were exchanging smiles and nods when the bailiff opened the door.

After they were seated and Judge Bannet explained about the sanctity of one's last will and testament he slit open the first envelope. It was Bill's document and the reading took five minutes. He left everything to his daughter Jessie, to do with as she saw fit. Patty never even batted a lash.

But she sat up a little straighter as the Judge slid the next, heavier envelope in front of him. He opened it and began, "I, Laverne Viola Tater, being of sound mind and sober temperament hereby make this, my last will and testament. My home and property, including all buildings located in Forest County at 41232 RTE 36 I leave to my stepson William Bradford Lyons, a more honest man I have never met."

"My daughters Tina and Patricia both married good men who have provided well for them and both have been successful in their professions. Tina, as an artist and Patricia, as a politician. They need nothing from me, but to Tina, I leave my grandmother's dining room set. I know she always loved it and will care for it. To Patricia, I leave her grandfather's walnut credenza. Hopefully, it will look good in the governor's mansion someday."

"My blessed grandchildren however are young, with their lives ahead of them. To my three grandsons James, Jacob and Jubal, I leave a sum of twenty five thousand dollars each. Use it wisely. To my granddaughter Jessie, who always had time for an old lady and shows such good promise I bequeath all remaining property, assets and personal belongings." With that the Judge laid the paper aside and said they were finished.

"Mrs. Smith, you will remain after I dismiss this hearing. Do you have an attorney?" she shook her head and looked at Ollie White. "Your Honor, I must recuse myself, as I am on retainer to Mrs. Lyons."

Judge Bannet nodded his head, "Mr. Fontana, in order to expedite matters will you agree to be temporary council for Mrs. Smith?"

Joe Fontana rose and said, "I will, your Honor."

"In that case I declare this matter settled, Godspeed everyone."

Patty didn't move a muscle, it was as if the old bitch had reached out and slapped her from beyond the grave, (which may have been the intension). Ollie White took her arm and led her out of the room. He closed the door.

Judge Bannet looked at Jessie and Attorney Fontana, "Mrs. Smith, your grandmother made a detailed list of all properties she owned. There will be a delay in your obtaining title to the house, business, and land that had been bequeathed to your father which he in turn left to you. Do you understand?" She nodded. "It is simply formalities that Mr. Fontana can easily explain to you at some later time."

The Judge pursed his lips and picked up another piece of paper, "In Venango County there are fourteen separate parcels of land. Nine with structures, two under rental agreement, and five, that are undeveloped. In Forest County there are thirty two separate properties, twenty six with structures, four under rental agreement, and six that are undeveloped. She had set up a separate account at the bank that will pay the taxes on all those properties perpetually. Once again, Mr. Fontana can explain this at some later time."

He cleared his throat and took a sip of water, "The total amount of acreage in Venango County is four hundred and twelve acres. In Forest County there is one thousand seven hundred and fifty six acres." Jessie's eyes were wide and her lips were pressed together. "In the Frontier Bank, along with the aforementioned account is her separate, personal account of five million, eight hundred seventy seven thousand, five hundred and thirty two dollars and seventy six cents, also, there is this key. He handed her a small key on a loop of yarn. "A safety deposit box key is what she told me."

Jessie's hand was shaking as she accepted the bit of yarn in her palm. "Young lady, you and your husband need an attorney. Your grandmother was a shrewd business woman, shrewd and honest, a successful combination. She was also my friend, I will miss her."

"I, I... oh Grammy..." Jessie burst into tears. "Good luck, young lady." The judge rose and left the room.

Chapter Nine

Patty had never felt like this in her life. She had foreseen every outcome but the one that happened. Millions of dollars on the line and that crazy old bitch of a mother of hers had screwed her royally. She tried to think, but all she could see in her mind was Dougie telling her how their future hinged on her controlling that property of the old Holmren place.

There was a one point five million dollar bonus on the lease signing she saw slipping out of her hands. She was so close, damn, damn, damn, DAMN!! She stopped, lit a cigarette. She leaned against Jessie's Jeep. She began to think.

Settle down, you're smarter than everybody else. Now, get your shit together and think. She blew a cloud of smoke in the air. She would have to manipulate her daughter. How? She smiled. She would break every rule in the politician's handbook. She would tell the truth. She relaxed, took a deep drag on her smoke and waited on Jessie.

Joe Fontana waited until Jessie regained control of her emotions then escorted her to the ladies room so she could clean up. Jessie washed her face and then stared in the mirror. She thought how delighted her grandma had been when she finally learned how to crochet. How hard it had been when the old woman had been sick and Jessie had to help her in the bathroom.

Her mother rarely asked how Grandma was, forgotten like an old couch in the back room. Heck, her mother hardly took any interest in any of them. She only called when she needed something, and never wanted her family anywhere near Harrisburg. She resolved to do the best she could with Laverne's legacy.

Attorney Joseph Fontana was waiting patiently for what he hoped would be his new client. He would introduce her to Janet Rapp who was now working as a junior partner out of his office. Janet had been educated at Smith University in Massachusetts and was now in her second year of practice. The fees would go through his account and he was sure he could make a tidy amount with little effort. Yes indeed, Mrs. Smith would be a good asset. Ollie could keep the senator.

Jessie came back into the hallway. "Jessie, there are several things you have to do as soon as possible. When I return to my office I'll write a list and then I'll have my junior partner, Miss Rapp, call you tomorrow and make arrangements."

Jessie nodded, "I'm a little overwhelmed right now. I really need to think about all this."

"That is perfectly understandable, Janet will call you tomorrow afternoon and you two can work things out." Fontana smiled and put his hands in his pockets.

When she walked out of the courthouse she saw her mother standing by her car. She was talking with two other ladies. "... and the way you are handling these double tragedies, commendable."

"Why thank you Mrs. Branch, it has been difficult as you can well imagine." Patty's hand went to her bosom.

"Oh you're more than welcome Senator, please remember that the DAR stands firmly behind the prettiest senator this commonwealth has ever had," Mrs. Branch gushed as her companion nodded gravely.

"What a nice compliment, I do appreciate your support. Oh, here's my daughter Jessie, say hello dear." Patty was smiling like a person in awful pain struggles to put on a brave face.

"How do you do ladies," Jessie said as she searched for her keys.

"We're both fine dear, we can't wait until you apply for membership in our organization," Mrs. Branch touched her on the hand.

Patty spoke up as Jessie stared at the two matrons, "My, how much we would love to chat but there is pressing business we must attend to. These deaths have certainly caused an awful lot of disruption in our lives." With that they got in the Jeep and pulled away.

They didn't speak on the way home but Patty was acting nevertheless. She stared out the window, wringing her hands, sighing at certain points. Jessie wasn't paying much attention, not only was she driving but her mind was still trying to comprehend what had just happened. Patty was getting pissed, she didn't like being ignored.

"Jessie, take the next right back to the Pithole Memorial. I want to show you something."

Jessie did as she was bidden with no questions, still in a form of shock. They pulled up into the parking lot of the site and stopped. Patty let the truth out, not the whole truth being a politician mind you, but enough to widen Jessie's eyes.

"... and the remainder of the Holmren farm and the old Yoder place are now yours. I tried to buy those off her and she had agreed to think about it. I'm sure she would have but she never had enough time, my poor mother. Anyway the deals are set and it would be a crushing blow, not only to me but the local economy and the state. Think of the high paying jobs this will bring in. I need to control those properties, besides they only want to make an exploration."

Jessie shook her head, "Mother, for such a smart person you can do some stupid things," she sighed, "let me sort things out for a week or two. I can't promise anything right now, but you are my mother." At that moment the baby kicked for the first time.

Dwayne couldn't believe his ears later on at dinner, Patty had left and it was just the two of them sharing a frozen pizza. "You mean we're rich," he said as his pizza slice was halfway to his mouth.

"It's a fact, don't know exactly how much everything is worth but the bank account alone means we will never have to worry how we're gonna pay the bills." Jessie picked up another slice and pointed it at Dwayne, "Now I can understand why she had me take all those courses in business stuff." She told him about the conversation she had with her mother and Dwayne replied that Patty might be trying to pull a fast one, but Jessie assured him she would never sell the property to her.

"I may rent it to her or something but I'm not going to worry about all that until I have a clear view of things," she said, Dwayne could only agree.

The next day at the State Police barracks Officer Bells handed a packet to Detective Sike, "Here's the pictures back from the lab that were in that camera we found." Sike took them and broke the seal on the envelope, sure enough, there were the girls posing for shots with wine coolers and what looked like a marijuana cigarette. Then at the end of the roll were a couple slightly blurred shots of a man with a wide grin looking in the window, his face almost touching it.

There was a computer disc enclosed and he put it in and brought up the pictures on the screen. "It looks like the car was in motion when these last two were taken. See how the brush was blurred?" Officer Bells nodded, "I also see that the man appears to be wearing a black hat and coat or something."

He enlarged the pictures on the computer to get better detail, "Let's look at that statement the truck driver made again," the detective read the statement, noting the description of the man they couldn't prove was there. "Could be the driver saw this feller, but there was no way he had ran over him like he said. That grin makes him look like a maniac. We need to talk to that driver again and I want to know where those kids got that alcohol." Officer Bells nodded and went out the door.

*****

The next couple of weeks were a whirlwind of activity for Jessie. She signed a lot of papers she didn't fully understand, putting her trust in Joe Fontana and Janet Rapp whom she came to like and admire. The two ladies traveled to see each property and meet the tenants of the rentals. Jessie assured them that the past agreements would be honored and the rent would not increase.

She realized she had a full time job on her hands and with the baby's impending arrival she would need some help. Dwayne had his hands full at the shop, working with Woody and the others. She hired Janet as her full time attorney and began to look for a domestic helper.

Patty called on a Sunday evening and informed Jessie she would be receiving a piece of registered mail containing papers to be signed concerning the property they had discussed. Patty told her that the best way to expedite things was to give her power of attorney and then Jessie could forget about them but still own them. She would also receive a nice check for her troubles as soon as the oil company was given the go ahead for the test drilling. She also told her how this would save her mother from any embarrassment and as this was a private family matter, she would not need to involve her attorney as all the legal ramifications had already been completed by the very best lawyers at the senator's disposal in Harrisburg.

"Jessie, those papers have to be signed and Fedexed back to me as soon as you get them. There is a deadline on this, and it is fast approaching. You can trust me on this; I am your mother and would never do anything underhanded to you." Jessie knew of course that her mother had never been aboveboard in anything, but she was her mother. She agreed, "Okay Mom, I'll do it, but only, ONLY because you're my mother."

"Don't worry dear, everything will be alright. I would never do anything against you, just wait until you get that check I promised, you will be rich." Patty hung up, leaned back and smiled.

Jessie hadn't told her how much money had been in the bank account she had inherited. As a matter of fact, she hadn't told her mother much about anything. It was puzzling that she hadn't asked, but then again, with the resources at her command she probably already knew everything. Jessie didn't know that Laverne had always let on to Patty that she was dirt poor and barely made enough to keep the roof over her head. Laverne had never let on she had anything and Jessie was shocked when she learned the truth. Jessie had learned from Laverne and volunteered nothing.

Jessie sat there for a few minutes with that bad feeling in her stomach that she had done something very bad. She still believed she controlled the situation. Then she thought, Mother never once asked how the baby was coming along, how Dwayne was. Nothing, oh well, that was her mother.

Two days later Patty held the papers in her hand and called Dougie. He set up a meeting with her and Mr. Hunt who had remained in Harrisburg. They signed the ninety nine year lease agreement giving Patty ten percent of all gas produced. Hunt personally signed a company check for one and a half million dollars and handed it to Senator Lyons with a smile. There were smiles all around.

Patty left. Mr. Hunt handed Dougie a briefcase with a nod. Dougie assured him he had Senator Lyons under complete control, he was told he had better. Events began to move. Patty had her secretary deposit the check and get a cashier's check for Jessie. She swung her chair around and looked out the window at the bright blue sky and felt a little giddy. One and a half mil and all perfectly legal, she smiled, she was on her way.

A few days later Jessie got a letter from her mother, it read; Jessie, here is your check from the lease business. Not a bad paycheck for signing a couple pieces of paper huh? I'll keep in touch, Mother. The check was for twenty thousand dollars. When Jessie got to the bank to deposit it she couldn't find her pen and started digging in her purse. Gum, file, paper, tissue, hair tie, paper, pen! She pulled it out and a piece of yarn was caught on it. The yarn was tied to a small key, she had forgotten about the key!

After depositing the check she asked the teller if that was a safety deposit box key and was assured that it was. She asked to open the box. The bank officer led her into the small secured room. Its walls were lined with six by nine inch doors and there was a tall table that stood alone in the middle of the area. The officer inserted the bank key in door 1044 and then the customer key. She placed the unopened box on the table, showed Jessie the button to push when she was through, then left the room, shutting the door behind her.

Inside on top was an envelope with her name on it, she placed it on the side. There were three stacks of hundred dollar bills, two diamond rings, four letters that grandpa had written from world war two, and wrapped in cellophane was a dried, red rose. She gazed at those items for a little while then closed the box, placed the envelope in her purse and pushed the button summoning the bank lady.

She waited until she got home and was alone before she opened it. " Dear Jessie, I must be gone now and Judge Bannet has given you the key. You were the only one who paid any attention to me and nursed me when I was sick. I thank you for that from the bottom of my heart, I love you very much. Do what you will with the fruits of my hobby. One thing though and this is very important. The land that was once the Holmren farm and the Yoder place? It should be posted and left strictly alone. There is a form of evil that haunts those properties. There were stories from way before I was born and many strange things have happened there in my lifetime. No good has ever happened there. Keep people off of it. Never sell or lease that property, and never go walking there by yourself. Other than that dear, enjoy your life, love your children and keep that wonderful husband of yours. I wish I could be there with you and who knows, maybe I will be. Love, Grammy."

Jessie read it three or four times, that bad feeling of apprehension invaded her stomach. She remembered the story of how the Jeep came to be hers and all the creepy things she had heard all her life about Pithole. She looked at the deposit slip laying there and thought what have I done?

Her mother had said they were only going to drill a test well and they probably wouldn't find anything anyway. Hadn't the place been abandoned because the oil had run out? She took the letter, and all the papers her mother had sent her to Janet Rapp, she hoped she could stop things. Janet shook her head at the development, but got to work finding out what she could do.

They changed Laverne's old room into a nursery, bright yellow paint with cartoon figures on the walls. Dwayne bought a new truck and the business got a new coat of paint as well. Jessie finally found some household help in the person of Miss Lydia Mae Plunk, a recent college graduate looking for a teaching job and not having much luck. They both were present at the interview and when Jessie ran out of questions Dwayne reached and shook Lydia's hand, holding it for an extra few seconds. He instantly saw her honesty and the goodness of her soul. He turned to his wife and said, "I believe this lady is who we should hire," and he gave Lydia a warm smile.

Jessie had learned that surveyors had been working on the old Holmren and Yoder places and that a bulldozer arrived and cut a new road into the property. Attorney Rapp filed a writ with the court and work was halted. That was when they found out who they were up against. A team of five attorneys representing Richardson Oil strolled into the first hearing and the injunction was overturned. Janet and Jessie were stunned, Janet, however, told Jessie she would work as hard as she could on this issue. What had put a shaft of solid steel in her resolve, was when one of the attorneys wearing a suit that had probably cost more than Miss Reno's car, gave her a smarmy smile with a snort of contempt that clearly said, "You're way out of your league little girl."

She had grown up with five brothers, her mother in a wheel chair and an absent father. She had cleaned, cooked, and took care of her mother. She worked hard at home, hard at school, and even with a partial scholarship she held two part time jobs the entire time she attended Smith, where almost all the other women there came from privilege and were there simply to appease their parents. Jessie had no idea what a fierce competitor she had sitting by her side.

In the meantime work continued and a site was readied for the drilling rig that was on its way from Oklahoma. Equipment and containers began to arrive. Three mobile homes were set up for an office and quarters for the overseers. They had to widen the road to allow access for the rig and take down power lines and close the historic site for two weeks.

The rig arrived on site the day that Starla Laverne Smith was born. Patty made an appearance at the hospital, looked at her granddaughter for a few seconds, said not a word to Dwayne or Jessie and left. She did appear at the drilling site and met with the press she had called in. She made a speech about how a new age of prosperity was dawning not only for the Venango and Forest County area but the entire state as well. There was no mention of the new addition to her family or the injunction that had been overturned. Patty didn't like the idea of being a grandmother, didn't like the idea of getting old.

Dwayne proudly handed his daughter to his mother to hold, "She's as healthy as a horse the doctor said," he remarked, as his mother made cooing sounds at the little bundle in her arms.

"And how is our new mother doing," Albinious smiled down at Jessie in her bed.

"They say everything went good and I should be out of here in a day or two," Jessie smiled as her picture was taken holding her daughter. No one mentioned her mother.

The next few weeks saw Jessie as a busy girl. Just keeping up with the baby's needs filled her days and Lydia proved to be invaluable with her help. However, when she saw the size of the drilling rig being set up and all the support equipment surrounding it, she realized that was no mere test hole they were drilling.

Janet Rapp dug deep into state law and found several clauses she could use to halt the project. She told Jessie that lifting a power of attorney status was very difficult and against someone like her mother, damn near impossible. However, there were environmental laws that were possibly being broken by this new form of exploration, and together they filed their next injunction. Work was halted.

At the rig site one of the mechanics was up on the upper platform checking welds and connections. He lifted his hardhat to wipe his brow and looked out over the area. He noticed a man standing in the tree line observing the site. He thought it odd the man was wearing such heavy clothes in the mild weather. He reached up and readjusted his helmet and when he looked at the place the man had been, he saw that he had vanished. He shrugged and went back to work.

Chapter Ten

Jessie and Janet returned to court and listened as the judge overturned the injunction. A new team of attorneys representing the interests of Senator Lyons had appeared and joined forces with the company lawyers. The judge gave them a withering look. His job had just become even more complicated. Work resumed.

Two weeks later Ms. Reno filed another writ, stopping the process as another hearing was granted. That evening Jessie received a phone call from her mother.

"What do you think you are doing?" Patty asked with venom in her voice, "Do you really think you and that country lawyer can keep this up, let alone win?"

"Mother." she sighed, "That is no test hole they are going to drill. Grandma left me clear instructions of what was to be done with that land, and if I had known those wishes at the time, I would never have given you any leeway about that property."

"Well you did, and there is nothing you can do about it. You will stop fighting this immediately, and put all this out of your mind. You did take the money I so generously sent you, so I see no reason for any further confrontations."

"You want the money back?" Jessie checked her recording device that Janet had insisted on her using for all calls about the well business. "I should sue you for even sending such a small amount, a ninety nine year lease? Really Mother, you are such a bitch."

"That is none of your concern. It will revert back to your heirs when it expires, so you can just go sulk all you want, you and that weak minded husband of yours."

"I've just begun to fight, good-bye Mother." She hung up and said to one at all as she clenched her fists, "Eeeeeewwwoo!!" It was only later that she realized that her mother had not asked one question about the baby.

Janet Reno became an expert at delaying actions, citing every reason she could think of for continuance after continuance. The court ruled against her over and over again, it was Judge Crocker's last case as he then retired and newly appointed Judge McBride took over the proceedings. Aiden McBride had spent twenty two years as the Venango County District Attorney. He was a no nonsense man and prided himself on his conviction record.

Two weeks later, Ms. Reno filed another injunction, citing environmental impact clauses in the state and federal law. The company lawyers were told to try a different tact. On Friday afternoon that week Judge McBride was greeted as he reached his car in the parking lot. He did not recognize the neatly dressed man as he approached carrying a briefcase. After a minute of conversation Judge McBride smelled a rat and told the man that he would not speak to him about any court matters outside the courthouse. He then asked the man to see him on Monday morning in his chambers before sessions began.

On Monday the man appeared and told the Judge after pleasantries how very interested the oil company was in a fair decision concerning this whole matter. He then offered the Judge a sum of fifty thousand dollars cash that could be used for a donation to the Judge's favorite charity.

"That smells of a bribe," Aiden McBride stated.

"Call it what you will, your honor and be advised there is plenty more cash available in the future," the man said with a satisfied smile.

Judge McBride held up a finger and said, "Hold on one moment please." He pushed a button on his desk and the Sheriff and one of his deputies entered the room. "Place this man under arrest, charge him with obstruction of justice, attempted bribery. Search him good and tell the jailer he may have something concealed on his person." The judge then reached behind himself and pushed back a curtain that had concealed his secretary and the court stenographer.

"Did you ladies hear the conversation?"

"Yes your honor and we have it conscribed."

"Very well, Sheriff, do your duty."

"This is entrapment," the astounded man shouted, "You can't do this."

"My court will not be compromised, tell that to your constituents."

The oil company attorneys denied any and all knowledge of the man. Nor did they acknowledge any part of a bribe. However, the way the law was interrupted was in favor of Richardson Oil. Work resumed.

The hundreds of jobs it would create as promised by Senator Lyons amounted to four security positions and ten part time truck drivers. Jessie became discouraged but Janet would not relent.

"We can fight this in more ways than one, if you wish to pursue this," Ms. Reno told Jessie.

Jessie looked at Dwayne and he told her to do what her heart told her to do. The ladies turned to the internet.

*****

In Harrisburg Douglas Cornet announced his bid for Governor and began his campaign. He had absolutely no plans to publicly align himself with Senator Lyons as he knew the story of her current problem was going to break and he told her that. He still saw her at the motel and assured her that when the problem was solved and forgotten he had big plans for her.

Patty wasn't stupid and went along. However, she began to see Mrs. Cornet and the two became friends, much to the chagrin of Mr. Cornet. He was amused; he thought it made things... interesting. Patty and Madeline attended fund raisers, went shopping, had several lunches and just got along swell. Patty had a plan.

Starla was growing. A happier baby was never born. Oh, she cried at the times all babies cry but she wasn't fussy and smiled and cooed whenever

Dwayne held her. She garnered a lot of Jessie's attention also, when Jessie wasn't busy doing all the things that made up her busy day.

"I never thought, that being rich was such a hard job," she said to Dwayne one evening as they snuggled in bed. Dwayne replied that he had a different hard job for her to do and she giggled as she turned to him.

In the old days when an oil or gas well was drilled down to the oil bearing sand, they would fracture the sand and release the oil which would then pool at the bottom of the well. This was done using dynamite at first but then a better way was discovered using nitroglycerine.

The shooter would construct a small platform right over the well head, using a plumb bob to properly align the dropping point. He then used a pulley system to carefully lower small jars of the volatile explosive to the bottom and stack them. Tricky work using the sense of touch on the cord. Then he would position a small rocket hanging from the platform and shoot it down the shaft, dangerous business. There weren't many old timers in that profession.

In modern times wells are much deeper and traditional fracking methods were obsolete. Now, they would perforate the pipe, put a pressurized cap on the well and force a mixture of sand, water and chemicals down the money hole, increasing pressure until the underground deposit fractured. "Hydraulic fracturing" was the new term.

What they didn't know or shrugged off was that the displacement process disturbed the ancient strata causing minor earthquakes, usually registering 3.0 or less on the Richter scale, which mostly went unnoticed by the general public. Minor cover-ups were not a problem and they kept on drilling ever deeper, learning how to drill horizontality.

At a mile underground they could send the shaft off to the right, or the left, or really, in any direction. They could reach areas that were forbidden to them from the surface, in effect, stealing the minerals from the unsuspecting public.

Dwayne came in the house at the end of the work day and told Jessie that their contract with the state highway commission was not being renewed. The next day they lost the state school bus account and a state health inspector arrived and failed their public facility, they were essentially shut down.

They had no choice but to lay off their employees all except for Woody, who was helping to renovate the restroom to bring it up to inspector's standards. Jessie knew this was her mother's work but Janet said there was little she could do.

Janet did however find a new reason to stop the drilling. Citing the Safe Drinking Water Act, she filed for disclosure of the chemicals used in the drilling and fracking process. Judge McBride halted work once again. Two weeks later a reform bill was attached to the act by congress, exempting the companies performing exploratory drilling from disclosure of means. This became known as the Halliburton Loophole.

Jessie contacted environmental groups such as "Earth First," the "Earth Liberation Front," and "Eco-Heros" they plastered the internet with posts of protest and alerted the general public to the plight happening in western Pennsylvania.

In a profound show of force the Rainbow People gathered in the nearby Allegheny National Forest and launched an all nude protest at the site, led by none other than their own Chrissie Moker, Pure Earth Goddess. They formed a long line, some holding signs, and some holding hands. The state police and the sheriff's department arrived and looked at the five hundred plus people assembled. After a long radio conversation with his superiors, Officer Bells raised his loud speaker and told the group that they were in violation of the indecent exposure law. Ms. Moker had her own voice amplifier and made the statement that the human body was created by God, and there was no indecency to it. Officer Bells replied that, that was a religious matter but they were in violation of state law regardless and subject to arrest. Ms. Moker then turned her back to the officers, and bending over said, "Now this is indecent exposure!" She was promptly placed under arrest along with twelve others and taken away. The news crews caught every second on camera. The remaining protesters scattered, but returned the next day.

This made national news, but any mention of Senator Lyons was hushed up in the media. After two weeks the group was asked to leave their camps in the national forest and cease their protest ranks. When they became slow in complying fire trucks were dispatched and the hoses turned on the hapless peaceniks.

This development did not make news anywhere, except for anti-media web sites that were ignored by the heads of the networks. Big money was swinging its big stick.

Judge McBride did the only thing he could do at that point and sent the whole matter to the state supreme court. Work would be delayed for at least two years.

Patty was incensed by this latest decision. Most of her money was still safe in the bank, but she had been counting on receiving royalties by now. That damn kid was holding her back. Elections were coming up. She needed to focus on campaign support for Dougie, who was making his bid for governor this year. She needed to go shopping for new clothing. She called Madeline, her new best friend.

Two days later Dougie told her he needed to relieve some of the stress he was feeling during his campaign. He produced a wolf mask for himself and a Little Bo Peep outfit for her. He told her to baa like a lamb as he mounted her from behind with the mask on and howled and growled.

Patty actually liked this, she felt like an actress. They began to pick costumes and themes for their trysts. Pirates and damsels, cavemen, king and queen, farmer and cow, Dougie seemed to really like doing it with a mask on, they were having loads of fun! Dougie had a new tone of confidence in his speech and a swagger in his appearances. His popularity polls soared, and all this was reflected on Election Day. A senior senator from Bucks County was chosen for the lieutenant governor's spot and the voters cheered.

Dougie assured Patty that she was going to be included in his next step up. Patty smiled; he was falling into her trap.

--- ---- ---

Two years passed, the State Supreme Court met and agreed that the matter deserved more study before proceeding on the case. Patty couldn't believe she was facing more delay; she had to insure this would be the last one.

David Sike retired from the state police after an outstanding career. The only blemish on his record was the unsolved death near Pithole. He didn't like being retired. He didn't like daytime TV; he felt he was wasting his time. One morning at his wife's insistence, he was cleaning out the closet when he found all his personal notes on the cold case. He decided to look at it once again; after all, he had plenty of time.

After reviewing his papers he decided to visit the scene. He drove to the lane off Pithole road only to find a locked barrier and a "no Trespassing" sign posted by the leasee, Richardson Oil and Gas Company. As a private citizen he had no authority to enter the property. He noticed that other than the gate being there, nothing else seemed disturbed. The drilling site was a quarter mile away.

He drove to the library in Tionesta, and using the computers there he read all the old newspapers which had accounts of the incident. He did this to refresh his memory on what else had been occurring at the time. Using the search option he found that there had been several disappearances and bodies found in the area dating back to the early 1800's. There were stories of even more odd occurrences before that, way too many for such a small place even spread out over time.

He was at home that evening mulling through his discoveries when the phone rang, it was Senator Lyons. "Hello Detective, I hope I'm not disturbing you."

"Just Dave now Senator, I'm retired from the force. How can I help you?"

"Well Dave, I have reason to believe that my granddaughter is being neglected or worse. Would you be interested in doing some private investigating?"

David stared at the phone in disbelief, "I don't have a license for that sort of thing, and I've never had any reason to suspect any of that business." He lived just a half mile from Lyons Garage and went there for all his auto work.

"I see," said Patty, "a license application could be expedited and I'm sure you don't condone child abuse. You would be doing me a great favor just to observe the child's daily schedule and give me the details. I will pay all expenses of course and pay you one thousand dollars a week for your trouble."

He coughed, "I'd have to think about it Senator, can I get back to you?"

"Yes, but don't wait too long. I need this matter taken care of as soon as possible, for the child's sake." She gave him her private number and told him to call in the evening.

Dave sat and stared at the number. Child abuse, no way. He had seen Jessie and Dwayne with their daughter many times and they always seemed happy. Why a daily schedule? He knew about the conflict between Jessie and her mother over the gas company. The court battle, and legal maneuvering. How the senator had touted the new era of prosperity for her district, and rode that horse to re-election. He looked at the cold case papers on the table. He thought about the Jeep that Jessie still drove, he sighed.

Jessie finally shut down her computer. She had been studying ecological findings and researching the past contaminations from the oil fields. It was late. Dwayne was sleeping on the couch with the TV tuned to some sports thing. She smiled as she looked down at him; she heard laughter coming from Starla's room and went to investigate.

She silently opened the door and saw the child sitting on the floor, close to her "Towmater" nightlight. She was playing with her dolls. They were dancing in the air in front of her.

Jessie gave a gasp and the dolls fell on the carpet. The little girl turned around and said, "Hi Mommy," with a sweet smile. Jessie stared for a moment and then regained her composure.

"What are you doing out of bed, all good little girls are sleeping now, having nice dreams." Jessie picked her up to tuck her back in.

"Want Ropey," Starla said, and reached out as the rope doll Woody had made for her flew to her hand.

Jessie forced herself to act normal and put the child clutching her doll back to bed, "There," she said, "now, you can dream sweet little dreams." She leaned down and kissed her forehead. She closed the door as she slipped into the hall. She made a pot of coffee and woke Dwayne.

She explained everything she had seen as Dwayne sat there, his mouth hanging open. 'You mean like she was controlling them with her mind? What do they call that, telekinesis or something?"

"Yeah, just like that. You think this has anything to do with your sight gift?"

He shook his head, "I don't know. I want to see her do it. Maybe then we can see something, I can touch her while it's happening." He stared at his wife, "This is some wild shit."

"No shit," Jessie gestured with her hands, "we will have to be very careful with her, oh hell, what about Lydia?"

He reached across the table and took her hand, "We will simply have to deal with it," He looked at the clock above the sink, "kinda late ain't it, why don't we go to bed?"

"Sleep?" Jessie rolled her eyes, "I don't think I can sleep right now."

"I didn't say anything about sleep, did I? You look really sexy when you're all perplexed."

"Oh really?" she got up, "Only a horny devil like you would want to do THAT, at a time like this."

He started to chase her down the hall, "Any time is a good time with you."

They were laughing in their room, Starla smiled in her slumber.

Chapter Eleven

The year passed quickly, Patty was good at planning long range tactics. Her goals were simple. Marry the governor, and then a run at the White House. First the governor had to become a widower, and she needed more money of course. When the stupid retired cop didn't call back, she called a man Dougie had mentioned once when they had been talking about covert operations, after watching a movie based on a Tom Clancey novel.

He asked if observation was all she wanted done, and when that was confirmed he named a price. She agreed then told him she would contact him when she was ready. She then called the lady who was the secretary of the DAR in Titusville. She told the lady she wished to surprise the first lady of the commonwealth with an award and thought a benefit dinner put on by her staunch supporters at the Titusville DAR would be appropriate. Twenty minutes later she received a call back giving whole hearted approval.

Patty gave them the specifics, "Remember, this is very important. No announcements that she will be there, otherwise she will hear of it, and we want this to be a complete surprise." She said in a light hearted manner. She hung up the phone and smiled, she had given them six months notice knowing they would never be able to hold a secret that long.

The gas company posted a bond with the state so they could continue support operations at the site. The Supreme Court met a month later and ruled in favor of the oil company, which was of really no surprise. The wheels had been well greased.

Drilling began again in earnest. They were soon finished and cemented the casing pipe. There were three shafts running out from the main hole, one to the east, one to the south, and one to the west. They would shoot all three shafts at once, creating a gigantic gas bearing pool. Mr. Hunt gave the order to commence fracking and leaned back at his desk outside Dallas. He smirked as he lit a forty dollar cigar, and began to think of that small island off the coast of Belize he was going to buy.

Starla was growing and learning. Lydia, who had been brought into their confidence when the child displayed her abilities, was amazed. This was no mere teaching job. Always, the emphasis was on Starla, first learning to control thoughts and emotions. She displayed a very high IQ and was reading at a second grade level after turning four.

To Starla, using her mind to control things was as natural as walking, but when Mommy and Daddy explained how it would frighten other people she understood the reason to hide it. However, she was a mischievous little girl and loved to play practical jokes. The cat learned to avoid her at all cost.

They found that she could manipulate objects at whatever distance, as long as she could see them. She absolutely adored Woody and he soon learned the secret also, she called him, "Poppy". One evening, they had been watching TV, when the movie "Firestarter" came on. Starla proved she also had that ability which frightened her mother. They had a long talk and Starla understood how some things must not be done when they could hurt anyone.

Later that night Dwayne brought up the end of the movie when the people had been discussing how much power the little girl had, and what the government had planned to do to her after they found out the extent of the child's ability. Jessie said, "Our daughter is not going anywhere near the government, total homeschooling for her, with patience, kindness, and love."

Dwayne thought about their teenage years and said, "We must teach her VERY well."

In September, Patty made the call to the man she had contacted. She provided him with expense money and gave him half his fee. He traveled to the area and rented a small apartment twenty miles from the house he would be observing.

He would arrive before dawn, parking his vehicle where it wouldn't be seen easily. Dressed in camouflage and perched high in a tree where he had line of sight, he was not noticed. Every day for three weeks he ascended to his spot and using binoculars and a telephoto lens, he remained there until evening. He noted in his report that every day except Sunday, the child was let out at three to play in the backyard with her swing set and playhouse for at least an hour, weather permitting, and usually alone. He took a lot of pictures and carefully recorded the time of each event.

Patty called Madeline and asked her about her schedule for the coming months. When she learned she had two free days at the end of October Patty told her that the DAR in Titusville was planning an award dinner for her, and asked if the first lady of the commonwealth would care to accompany her for publicity purposes. She added that it would solidify support for the governor in that part of the state, besides, it would be fun for the both of them to take a mini vacation together. Madeline agreed, and when she learned it would be an overnight stay for the two of them, became enthusiastic. Patty smiled. She went out the next day and purchased a full sized Lincoln.

****

Dave Sike pulled his Explorer in the garage. Woody guided him onto the lift and held up his hand to halt him, "Let's see the lights and toot the horn." The Ford was due for its safety inspection. "Ok," said Woody, "high beams, turn signals. Good let it blink. Wipers please." Woody walked around to the back, "Brakes, flashers, okay, you can get out now."

Dave shut the door and walked over to the office. Dwayne and Jessie were both in there, after the pleasantries and such, he asked about their daughter.

"Oh she's just fine," said Jessie smiling her best, she had always liked the former detective. "She's up at the house with her tutor right now."

"Oh, that's good, umm, how's your mom doing?"

Jessie told him she must be doing okay, but they haven't had much contact in the last couple years. She added that all those campaign pictures of a happy, smiling family were a bunch of malarkey. Dave nodded but added nothing.

Woody stuck his head in the door, "Get his paper work going, he's good for another year. I'll go wash up and be right in to sign the new sticker."

Dave handed over his insurance card and registration, "You folks notice any strangers hanging around lately? I heard there may be some traveling burglars in the area, casing out country businesses to rob."

Dwayne looked up, "No, can't say I've noticed anything out of the normal run of campers and such." Jessie shook her head, "I haven't noticed anything, but then we don't get out much."

Dave nodded as he paid his bill. "Okay, just checking. Lot of crazies out there anymore." He had figured that the senator had been concerned that her granddaughter hadn't been enrolled in kindergarten. She had access to all the state records and had probably checked. "Oh, by the way, how's the court case coming along?"

Jessie frowned, "Not good, it really tore this family apart. It's sad you know, apart on seeing Starla when she was born, Mom hasn't once asked about her. We haven't seen her in over four years now. I don't think there is much more we can do as far as stopping the gas company, no matter what. My attorney says there is only one more avenue we can pursue, I haven't decided on that yet."

Dave was thinking as he got in his car, where did the idea of abuse come from? Why did she want to know the child's daily schedule? Something was nagging at him in the back of his mind.

****

Lydia Mae Plunk was laughing with Starla as the girl drew a smiley face, then a frowny face, a surprise face, and then a crying face. She truly loved teaching the child and had no regrets of taking the job of household helper four years ago. The pay was good and now she was living at the house. Jessie and Dwayne had become great friends.

"Yes, very good Starla. Now, let's do a mean face like this," Lydia made the appropriate facial pose. Starla giggled as she got a new piece of paper.

"Now, we start with a..."

"Big circle," Starla finished. She drew a decent oval and placed the eyes, nose, mouth, and ears on the paper. She paused for a second and drew in the inclined eyebrows to finish off the emotion. Jessie walked in the room at that point.

"It appears your daughter has another special gift." Lydia smiled, "Look at this art work."

Jessie laughed as she looked at the drawings, "Starla, you can be the next Charles Shultz."

"Who's that?"

"You know, the man who drew Snoopy and Charlie Brown. But now we need to clean up all this mess and get ready to make Daddy dinner."

Soon the three ladies were in the kitchen, "I am not too surprised at her talent," Jessie said to Lydia, "did you know her great aunt is Tina Lamont?"

"The artist, oh my, now I know where that comes from."

"Not from me, that's for sure. I can barely draw a bath." They both started laughing while Starla busied herself playing with a potato.

At that same time the gas company was shooting the perforating guns. Blasting holes through the last sections of the casing pipe into the gas bearing shale. This was in preparation for the forcing of the fracking mixture of water, sand, and chemicals to complete the job. In early October that step was completed and the final process was begun.

Patty finished reading the report and studied the photographs her hired man had compiled. A wry smile formed on her lips as she realized her plan taking shape. She was thinking about her daughter, how Bill always seemed to love that kid more than her. He should have been paying attention to me, she thought. No, second fiddle now, I was just the person he slept with. I wish I had never had that damn kid. Oh well, she's gonna get hers soon enough, right where it hurts. That will stop all the court nonsense, I'll begin collecting my money, and things will fall into place. The power of the White House will be mine. She picked up her phone and called the man, there was one last task for him to do.

****

That evening, David Sike couldn't concentrate on the TV, he was restless. He always got that way when something wasn't right, and his sub-conscious nagged at him. The next morning he decided to go for a little ride. Observe, is what the senator wanted him to do. He knew Patty was persistent, she would have found someone else to do her bidding.

He drove slowly around on the back roads surrounding the home and business. He wasn't sure what, exactly he was looking for but he knew it would be something out of the ordinary. He caught something out of the corner of his eye and stopped. He backed up. There was an old logging access road that had seen some recent use, he pulled in and parked.

There were several tire tracks which appeared to have been made by the same vehicle. He locked his Explorer and walked back in. he found where a vehicle had been parked and turned around several times. He began walking in ever widening circles until he spotted a tree that the bark had been scarred from repeated climbing.

There were a few gum wrappers laying around, all the same brand. Bingo. He judged that someone high in the tree would have a good view of the Smith home. Now, the big question, why?

Kerri Karson had been a keystone kid, a scholarship to Penn State then on to M.I.T. She was the engineering supervisor of the well and fracking operation. She had actually helped to develop the process. So far, everything had gone smoothly. The delays had been of benefit to her, as she had lots of time to check and double check each aspect of the job at hand.

Four long years of flights back and forth, she had rented an apartment in Titusville that the company paid for. It was a good job with great benefits. She was concerned about all the minor earthquakes that were occurring in Oklahoma that seemed to happen with every frack, but as they were so slight as not to cause public alarm, she followed company policy. She was studying on a way to keep the lower sub-strata stable but had not been able to figure it out yet.

This would be a big feather in her hat, the first deep Marcellus well in Pennsylvania. She saw the opportunity to be able to move back home to these hills and forests she loved and dearly missed. She hated Texas where it was so damn flat and hot. If this well was successful there would be many more and a stable future. She smiled as she read another report.

****

The creature could feel the minute vibrations and changes in the pressure as this new thing was happening. It decided to wake itself for a while, just in case. It had almost forgotten what real food was like. Though the energy it absorbed through its avatars was satisfying, there just wasn't any taste.

It would need some energy to stretch its muscles and change position, it decided to hunt. The man Patty had hired found the access road she had told him about. There was a gate with a lock. He cut the lock opened the gate and pulled his Subaru in, he shut the gate and put a new lock in place. He had mailed the senator one of the keys to the replacement.

He drove back in and found the place that a Roadrunner had parked so long ago. Using his new GPS device he determined that he was about a quarter mile from the property he had observed. He climbed a tree and set up a motion camera. He chuckled to himself, the senator was so stupid. Not only did he know who she was, now he would have evidence of whatever she was planning on doing. Blackmail could be very profitable.

He climbed down and stepped back to admire his handiwork, he smiled. He turned around and the man in black stood there with a wide grin. He never had time to scream. Two days later Patty opened an envelope and a key dropped out. The note inside confirmed that her last task was completed and the man was ready to meet her and get paid.

Patty called his cell phone but the call went through to voice mail. She sent him a quick text. She waited... nothing. Perplexed, she decided to wait for him to contact her. He would want the rest of his money and she had the 38 caliber bonus ready she was going to give him.

Chapter Twelve

"Higher, Daddy, higher," Starla squealed in delight, as Dwayne gave her a shove. He was laughing, "Hold on tight or you'll go sailing." The late afternoon sun was shining down and turning the colored leaves on the trees into iridescent wonders. Jessie was watching them play from the kitchen window, a pleasing smile on her face. While she was rinsing the potatoes she was thinking how strange, and yet how well her life has turned out.

Dwayne had told her earlier that Woody had coughed up a little blood at the end of work today, and that he was going to the hospital tomorrow to get checked out. She was hoping it wasn't serious, but damn, coughing up blood? Not good. If they lost Woody for any length of time they may as well close the shop. She thought of her daddy. Well, did they really need it? She put the spuds on to boil.

Starla had tired of the swing, and had run over to her pink and lavender, plastic, princess playhouse. Dwayne was doing a big bad wolf thing and Starla was laughing and squeaking. Jessie stuck her head out the back door and called them in to wash up, the sunset was beautiful.

At that moment the fracking fluid was being pumped in the well, water truck, after water truck were lined up and pumping in their mixture of brine water and chemicals. Chief Engineer Eillie Barns was pleased with the progress so far, on schedule and running smoothly. This would take a couple days, and with a notice to the new shift coming on to call her with updates she left for her apartment.

The danger time for earthquake activity she had observed, was right after the frack and they had pumped all the fluid out. She couldn't think of a way to avoid that. The shale had to collapse to release the gas and oil, and that displaced the strata. Still, the worst one had shown only 4.1 on the Richter scale and was barely noticeable. It had collapsed a few wells and cracked a few foundations. The company had no problem fixing these problems. Good public relations. Of course, that had been in North Texas and Oklahoma, the geology in Pennsylvania was a whole new ballgame.

The trapped creature was fully alert now. It was observing the well activity with a couple avatar black snakes in the trees. It thought the work the humans were doing was interesting, whatever it was. The energy it had absorbed from its latest victim coursed through its body. It flexed its muscles, its scales moving like smooth waves.

At the time of Jessie's conception it had caused a little extra something to appear in Patty's womb. It attached itself to Bill's sperm cells and an added thread of DNA mixed with the fertile egg. It was sure it could accomplish this, passing on some aspect of itself to the surface. The urge for even a small aspect of itself to survive was very strong. Jessie Jayne grew up with no evidence of this tiny bit of extra blueprinting. However, as in so many other inherited traits it skipped a generation.

The creature could create images to lure its prey, absorb remotely, the life energy collected by its avatars and preform simple telekinesis. Of course it had no way of knowing how this would interact with a human brain. Had it and the others of its species survived the eons of time to evolve, the Earth would be a very different planet. The fact, that neither Patty, nor Jessie gave birth to a reptile like child caused it to think it had failed. It did have several hundred fertile eggs in its womb and now it felt there might be a chance to lay them in the ocean. Freedom, it thought as it rippled its muscles one more time. Life.

*****

Patty guided her powder blue Continental up the drive to the Governor's mansion early. Madeline was almost ready and in good spirits. The house butler carried her suitcase to the Senator's sedan. He thought it odd that the trunk was lined with plastic sheeting, but after depositing the bag he closed the lid and gave it no further thought. His experience was that most politicians were a little odd.

Madeline, of course had inquiries made and found that the DAR of Titusville was indeed planning a festive dinner for her new friend. She was excited about the overnight excursion. Her role as the Governor's wife kept her tied to a tight, boring schedule. This was a bit of freedom, almost a lark. Famous people lose a great deal of anonymous freedom in their lifestyle.

"I am so glad to be getting away for a while," said Madeline, "Doug was planning on having me accompany him for a very boring evening with the agriculture secretary. Trust me, there's no culture in agriculture."

"I know what you mean," Patty smiled, "too bad we can't just keep going, do a Thelma and Louise thing."

"Good God, don't drive us off a cliff!" Madeline laughed.

Yak, yak, yak, as they continued on, the conversation turned to husbands. "Were you happy with your late husband?" Madeline asked.

"Happy? Pretty much at first, after I had our daughter something changed. He totally fell in love with that girl and I got displaced." Patty shifted positions behind the wheel, "He was a decent man, although he had no ambition. He was content to run his little business; once again, I was second fiddle."

"Did he ever cheat on you?"

"Bill, heavens no, like I said, no ambition."

"I wish Douglas were like that," Madeline sighed.

Patty turned her head, there were butterflies in her stomach, "What, no ambition? He wouldn't be the Governor without it."

"No dear, cheating. Dougie makes Bill Clinton look like a castrated monk."

Patty's acting mode kicked in. "Doug?" Patty said with her mouth open, "You know he cheats?"

"He started right after the honeymoon. There have been hundreds of women, some girls. I've suffered through many conversations with spurned girlfriends trying to hurt him."

"Oh my God, yet you stayed married to him, why?" Patty felt a little sick.

"Oh I have my little secrets too," Madeline shifted in her seat now facing Patty, "which is why I jumped at this chance to get away with you. Maybe we could become a little more... intimate." Madeline said as she placed her hand on Patty's thigh.

Patty almost burst out laughing; she put her hand over Madeline's and said, "You never know." As she turned off the interstate and headed north to Forest County, she was thinking about the tight string she was going to wind around Dougie's balls once they were married.

*****

Retired Detective David Sike stopped at the logging trail road, he saw no fresh tracks. He drove back home and called the Senator's office. He was going to say that he had reconsidered her proposal, just to see what she would say. The secretary informed him that Mrs. Lyons was out of town on her way to Titusville for a couple days. He hung up.

He mulled over what he knew. Jessie Smith, the now wealthy daughter of the Senator was at odds with her mother who had made some deal with the gas company. The Senator had only seen the child once. She had wanted to learn the child's schedule clandestinely. Why?

Evidence shows that someone, who quite possibly was still in the area, got that information to the Senator. What was Patty Lyons up to? He thought, he got up and changed into cammos and put on his hunting boots. He loaded and strapped on his 357 magnum and prepared to do a little surveillance himself. He put a couple snacks and a soda in his game cooler, along with his binoculars, plus a couple quick loads just in case. He walked into the woods, and headed for the Smith house.

*****

As Patty turned on route 36 to Titusville, she told Madeline she was going to show her the Marcellus gas well she was responsible for. Madeline nodded, she was curious. Patty turned on Pithole Road and drove past the Historical Site to the gated lane and pulled up to the barrier.

"Why are we here," asked Madeline, "I don't see anything."

"This is my very private place," Patty smiled at her, "no one around. We can be totally alone in here." Madeline had that look on her face that said, "Hmmm... this could be interesting."

Patty got out and used the key she had been sent, it worked. She drove through and re-secured the gate. "Bill and I came back in here before we were married, had lots of fun back here."

She drove back in, the bushes scraping the sides of her car. She was surprised to find another car back there, a brown Subaru. The turnaround was blocked. Patty shut off the engine and got out. This wasn't part of the plan. The car had leaves, small branches, and bird poop all over it. It had been there for a while.

"Hello, hello," she called out, silence was her reply.

She keyed the trunk lock and opened it. Madeline got out and stood by her door, "Maybe this isn't such a good idea?"

"We're fine," Patty opened the lid and pulled out her overnight case, "come see what I got in the trunk, you'll love it."

Madeline walked to the back of the car, "I don't know, Patty. I really don't like this."

"You won't like this much either." Patty said, as she pulled her revolver out of her case and pointed it at Madeline.

Patty...what in the..."

"Shut up, push your suitcase back and climb in, now!"

"Have you gone crazy...Patty?"

"Do it NOW." Patty thumbed the hammer back, "Or I'll shoot you in your goddamned face."

Shaking from fear and confusion, Madeline did as she was told, she just fit.

"Hands behind your back bitch," Patty said as she produced a pair of handcuffs, "just pretend it's some kinky lesbo thing." Patty locked them on and got out a roll of duct tape with pink ducks printed on it and did her feet and secured a rag in her mouth, getting the tape caught in her hair. Madeline started shaking her head no and making grunting noises. Patty reached down and squeezed her nostrils shut.

"Lay there quiet and still Madeline or I'll tape your nose shut." She quit struggling, tears streaming out of her eyes. Patty stood back, gave a little smile, "I'll be gone a little while, then I'll be back and we can take a little walk." She slammed the lid.

She pulled a pair of cammo coveralls out of the case and slipped into them over her pants suit. She tied her hair back and hid it under a matching ball cap. She looked at her watch, ten after two, she had plenty of time. She laced up her boots.

*****

Dave Sike was across the road from the garage and house. He was back far enough in the bushes to not be seen but had a decent view of the place. He couldn't see the whole backyard but he could see part of the swing set. He put down his cooler, set up his camp chair, uncased his binoculars and sat down. He wasn't even sure what he was looking for or if anything might happen, but he learned a long time ago to listen to his gut. The business was open and he could see Dwayne working on a Bronco. He saw Woody pull in and wondered where he had been.

Woody walked up to Dwayne and said, "It don't look good, they x-rayed my chest and the doc said my lungs look like a pair of raisins."

Dwayne's mouth fell open, "What, oh shit, that's horrible. You don't smoke, how can that be?"

Woody shook his head, "I told the doc that and he wants more tests, but he thinks it's from all the brake and clutch jobs I've done over the years. Asbestos, my friend, bad juju."

Dwayne made a face, "I'm positive the insurance will cover the medical, I'll check with Jessie to make sure. Don't worry Woody; we'll help no matter what."

"Oh, I know that, but I don't think money can fix this one," Woody picked up a wrench and stared at it, "nope, this looks pretty bad."

"I'll call Jessie at the house, she'll want to know."

*****

Eillie Barns was watching the gauges as the pumps began to run in reverse, sucking the fracking liquid out of the casings. She kept glancing at the seismograph also, even though it had an alarm set up. There was almost always an earthquake at this phase, usually only small ones that were never felt, but that was out west. The fluid was pumped back into a small fleet of water trucks then taken to large storage tanks to be saved for future use, a time consuming process.

The other techs in the office trailer watched their computers as the data came in. they too were apprehensive, all veteran employees. One of the geologists had argued that the strata was not as stable as what they were used to, too many huge rocks and underground springs. There were void places from all the old oil wells, just way too much water. The company had transferred him to Alaska.

*****

Jessie was helping Lydia clean the finger paint off Starla's hands. "...I agree Starla, pink is a very nice color for a kitty, but green eyes?"

Starla laughed at her mommy, "I like 'reen eyes."

The phone rang.

"Okay," Jessie said, "I'll be right there. Lydia, I have to go down to the shop, could you let our young Picasso out to play."

"Sure," Lydia nodded, "we'll be all cleaned up here in a couple minutes, then swing time." Starla giggled as she held on to Ropey the doll. Lydia dried her hands and reached for the door handle, "Come on kiddo, out you go."

Starla ran to the swings.

*****

Patty tensed, there's the kid she thought. She reached in her leg pocket and touched the zip lock bag that held the chloroform soaked cloth. She waited, her report said the kid would mess around with the swing set for a while then go in the pink plastic playhouse.

It was thirty feet from the wood line to the little house.

Perfect.

The Thirteenth Chapter

Starla climbed up the ladder to the top of the slide, holding onto Ropey with her teeth. Whoosh! She ran around and repeated the process. After several turns she ambled over to the playhouse and went inside.

Patty undid the zip lock on the baggie but held it tight shut. She ran hunched over to the side of the pink house and sprang around to the doorway on her knees. The child had her back to her as she grabbed her with her left arm while applying the chloroform with her right. After a few seconds the struggling stopped and the stupid homemade doll fell to the floor. Patty gathered her up and wasted no time in regaining the tree line and following the path back to her car.

Dave Sike watched Jessie exit the house and walk down to the garage. He saw Starla playing on the slide but that was all he could see of the swing set and backyard. He decided to move to where he could see it all.

Deep under the ground the pressure was abating as the fracking fluid was pumped out. The ancient fault slipped. Kerri Karson watched the pressure drop completely off the gauges then spike into the red. The seismograph's alarm went off and the shock wave hit. Kerri was knocked off her feet as the command trailer rocked and tilted. Alarms were sounding everywhere. She was terrified, this had never happened before.

She regained her feet and looked out the broken window to see a nine inch pressure hose whipping around spewing liquid. There were two men on the ground and not moving. Other men were running and shouting, total confusion and chaos. The well itself seemed secure though, as she replaced her hardhat and prepared to go out to inspect it up close. She was sure this was going to be big trouble.

The floor dropped away in the ancient cavern, the creature could move! It spun in a circle and detected the shaft. It started up, up to the surface, up to freedom. For a few seconds it couldn't understand what it was seeing, then, it realized, it was light.

Lydia had been coming down the stairs from the bathroom when the quake hit. She fell the last twelve feet and landed on her shoulder, she screamed.

The floor of the shop cracked with a loud snap and the office window shattered. Tools and equipment were scattered and thick dust blew in clouds through the bays. Jessie and Woody were in a glass covered pile on the office floor. Dwayne had held onto the desk top, he rushed to help his wife and friend brushing the broken glass away. Jessie got her wits about her, and picked her way back outside, then ran to the house, her ear bleeding from a cut.

Patty was about halfway back to her car. She wasn't used to physical exertion like carrying forty pounds of dead weight. She had slowed to a labored walk. The child fell out of her arms as she was thrown to the left as the quake hit, landing in a tangle of wild rose and thorn trees. Her face scratched and bleeding, her coveralls ripped. She extricated herself out of the natural barbs and grabbed the kid, saying, "shit, shit, shit," under her breath.

When she got back to her car she discovered a large red oak had fallen and crushed the cab and front of the Lincoln. She stood there dumbfounded. This was definitely NOT part of the plan! The child began to cough and move. She grabbed a handful of curly blonde hair and yanked its head back. She pulled out the evil smelling rag and dosed the brat again.

The trunk lid on the car looked twisted. She pushed the release on the key fob, nothing. She tried the key in the lock but it wouldn't turn. Now she was pissed. She needed Madeline to carry the kid, and she couldn't leave the damn bitch in the trunk of her car. She looked at the Subaru, the door was unlocked and there was a tire iron on the floor of the backseat. She'll open that flecken trunk.

Jessie ran in the house and found Lydia lying at the foot of the stairs. "Lydia! Oh my God, where's Starla?"

Lydia pointed with her good arm, "Out back by her swing, I think I broke something."

"Oh shit, hold on, hold on, I'll be right back," Jessie hopped over her microwave and sprinted out the shattered sliding glass door. "STARLA, STARLA, WHERE ARE YOU?" Nothing, no answer, she ran to the playhouse. No Starla, but Jessie spotted Ropey the doll laying on the floor, her stomach clenched up. She thought she smelt something funny also.

She stood up and faced the woods, "STARLA, STARRRRLAAA. ANSWER ME!" tears began as no answer came and she realized her baby was gone.

Dwayne came through the backdoor, "Jessie, where's Starla?"

Jessie turned and wailed, "She's not here, she's not here." Dwayne held her as she broke down, his eyes on the woods.

Woody was looking at Lydia Mae, he stood up and took her hand. "It's dislocated at the shoulder Honey, go ahead and close your eyes, I'm gonna make you more comfortable."

He placed his foot on her and yanked her arm. She cried out in pain and surprise, but the joint was back in its socket and was feeling better already. He grinned at her and said, "I was a medic in the Marines."

Sirens could be heard in the far distance as Dave Sike came around the side of the house and saw Dwayne and Jessie embracing by the little playhouse. He slogged up to them, out of breath, "Everyone ok? That was a damn earthquake, where's the little girl?"

Dwayne told him the child had been in the playhouse but was now missing. Dave stuck his head in and immediately smelled the odor of chloroform, then saw the forlorn doll. Jesus, he thought, kidnapping.

He stood up, "Has anyone looked in the house for her? She could have gone back in before the quake." Jessie ran to the house and got Woody and Lydia to help search.

Dwayne pointed at the doll, "She doesn't go anywhere without that doll, something happened." They both turned to the tree line.

Patty wasn't having much luck. The jack handle slipped and she hit the side of her face on the side of the car. She swore, she backed up and swung the tool out of frustration, banging the lid. It popped open.

Madeline was staring wide eyed and shaking. Patty cut the tape on her legs and un-cuffed her. Pointing the pistol at her eye she said, "Get out." It took a little time for that. Madeline's legs were asleep and she was disoriented from the slam she took when the tree fell on the car. Her hose were torn and she had wet herself.

Patty laughed at her condition, "Not so high and mighty now, are you?"

"Mmmmphhh, mmmmphhh," Madeline tried.

"Shut up. Pick up that damn kid, we're going for a little walk, remember?" Patty waved the gun.

The three searchers came out the back door and joined the detective and Dwayne. Starla wasn't in the house. Dave Sike spoke up, "We have to look for tracks, disturbed leaves, is there any paths leading back into the woods?"

Jessie ran to the path that she and Mary Bowser had used so many years ago, there, just a few feet along lay a little blue shoe. "That's her shoe!" yelled Jessie.

Dave said "Okay', and turned to the others, "someone has to stay here in case she comes back by herself." Lydia volunteered. Dave tried his cell but there weren't any bars, "Looks like the tower's down, the power is out too. Lydia, try the phone in the house and call the state police if you can. Tell them there has been a possible kidnapping. We're on our own for now, let's go." Jessie led the way up the path, Dave cautioned her on not calling out, as to alarm the kidnapper into doing something rash. They hurried along as best they could.

Madeline wasn't doing so good. She had never worked a day in her life and rarely exercised. Carrying forty pounds of dead weight through the woods in low heeled pumps was sheer torture. She stopped, lowered the child to the ground and pulled the tape and rag away from her mouth. She gasped for air.

Patty needed a breather also. She had thought their destination was closer. "That kid still breathing?" she asked Madeline.

"What? I don't know, yes, yes, her chest is moving. Patty what the ..."

"Shut UP." Patty needed to think, her plan had come undone with the loss of her car. She had noticed the keys in that other car though, hopefully it would start. First though, she was still going to dispose of her dear friend Madeline down that creepy old hole back in the woods a little ways. She might want to keep the kid for insurance. Problems, problems.

Twenty feet from the surface the shaft narrowed to a tight squeeze. The creature was tired. Its muscles had long gone unused and were painful. It decided to rest for a little while. It could breathe oxygen again. Its body began to metabolize to surface conditions. Its mind became sharper as a wave of reawakening pulsed through its body. It could sense odors once again, marveling at them, as if experiencing them for the first time, there were faint sounds also. It had sorely missed direct stimulation. The sounds drew closer.

"Far enough Madeline, put the kid down," Patty said.

Madeline sank to her knees and gratefully laid Starla on the leaves. She was breathing hard, sweat streaming down her face. "Patty, what..." she gasped and caught her breath, "what are you doing? Why are you doing this?"

Patty pointed the gun, "Get up and walk over there." Patty motioned toward a dark opening in a large cluster of rocks. Madeline got up on legs trembling with fatigue and took a few ungainly steps.

"Go on, get over there," Patty stepped forward, inadvertently kicking a few leaves on Starla's face.

Madeline stumbled on, she came to the rocks and saw the gaping hole and stopped. She turned to face her antagonist.

Patty raised the gun and said, "That's what we call the shortcut to hell. You can drop rocks down that hole and never hear them hit anything. It's a good place to make things disappear, go on, jump in."

"Have you lost your mind?" Madeline was mad now.

Twenty feet below in the stygian darkness, two eyes focused on the sounds.

"Shut up Madeline, jump in or I'll shoot."

"Oh my God, is this about Douglas? How stupid are you?"

"With you gone," Patty said with gleaming eyes, "he and I will wed, and go on to the White House."

"You actually believe that? Doug and I have no secrets. He calls projects like you his 'little games'. He played you like a fine violin."

"Projects, games? What are you talking about?"

Madeline began to smile in a rueful way, "That's right, a project. He delights in telling me all the sordid details, the sex, the pillow talk, the slow manipulation. Ha, he made untold amounts of future political contributions and a half mil in cash off you. Not to mention the priceless films. You ever wonder why, you and he always went back to the same room in that motel? No, you wouldn't, you're so naïve. He had cameras set up, from all different angles. I'll never forget the first real good one where you had that stupid bonnet on baaing like a little lamb, but, but, the best one was when you had that cowbell on your neck and kept going, 'mooo, moooo'. Oh my God, I pissed the bed. We had to buy a new mattress. He would never marry you, you gullible idiot."

Patty shot twice. The force of the bullets knocked Madeline over the rim, she vanished. She was still alive when she fell into the creature's mouth. It moved its jaws and crushed every bone in her body and swallowed the soft mass.

The taste of blood and body fluids was indescribable. Energy flowed instantly through its body as it absorbed the life force. Its first stomach swelled with the large meal.

*****

The path led them to the two cars. They stopped to check them out. Dave looked up from peering in the Lincoln, "Empty, nobody got hurt here."

"The trunk smells like pee," Dwayne said, "and there's a suitcase in there."

Dave walked back to the rear and saw the empty overnight bag with a roll of designer duct tape and a pair of women's shoes on the ground beside it. He glanced at the trunk and noticed the pry marks by the lock.

Woody was looking at the Subaru, "Looks like this thing has been here for a while, at least a week." Retired Detective Sike looked at the tread on the tires of it, pretty much a match of the ones of the logging road.

Jessie was getting frantic, "We got to find Starla, it's obvious she isn't here. We're wasting time, which way do we go?"

Dave tried his cell phone again but still no service. He looked around, "We have to see if we can find their trail. Everybody look around."

Dwayne found Starla's other shoe a few feet away, "Here! They must have gone this way."

"This leads back to the hole, Dwayne," Jessie said, the fear in her voice plain to them all.

They hurried along. Their heads jerked up when they heard the two shots. They were very close and ran ahead. They all saw the scene at the same time. Patty, with a gun in her hand turning back towards Starla, who was now trying to get to her feet.

"FREEZE, POLICE! DROP THE GUN!!" Dave roared as he aimed his pistol.

Jessie was shocked as she realized that was her mom with the gun in her hand. "MOM," Jessie yelled, "What are you doing?"

Starla was on her feet but wobbling, she started towards her mother. Patty raised the gun. Dave Sike couldn't shoot. The child was in the way. "MOM," Jessie yelled again. "DROP IT, DROP IT," Sike kept yelling. Patty fired once right at the retired police officer but missed, only to hit Dwayne who fell like a ton of bricks. Woody ran to him.

Jessie got another shock when the creature emerged from the cavern right behind Patty. It rose thirty feet straight up. Its head was the size of a mini-van, a fan like cowl rose behind its head. Its body was twelve feet thick and covered in gleaming black scales. Everyone but Patty looked on in awe.

Patty now pointed the gun at Jessie, who screamed, "RUN STARLA RUN!" Patty swung the gun towards the child and Dave Sike fired, hitting the senator in the shoulder, the gun fell from her hand. The creature struck straight down on Patty biting her off at the knees, then raised its head in the air. There was a muffled scream and a crunching sound and then she was no more.

Starla fell into her mother's arms. The creature paused and looked around at the forest. The last time it was free this had all been under the sea. It must get to water soon, but first, a feast would be just fine.

Woody spoke up, "The bullet grazed Dwayne's head, he's unconscious and he's bleeding like hell!" He continued to press down his handkerchief.

Dave raised his handgun and yelled at Jessie, "When I fire take the girl and run."

At that moment a man dressed all in black appeared in front of him and began to grin. Then one on either side of the first one, then another and another, soon there were at least a dozen of them surrounding the rescuers. Dave pointed his gun back and forth. Jessie, holding the crying child, stepped in closer to him. Woody stood up with a stick in his hand, ready to defend his fallen boss and friend.

The creature began to nod its head and the men in black started to dance sideways, back and forth, grinning like mad. The creature was having a little fun. Sixty percent of its body was still in the hole. The food had made its way down to the first stomach where powerful bile like juices began to break down the mass. The belly swelled and was now too large to pass through the narrow opening where the creature had paused before.

As the men shuffle danced they moved a little closer. Dave Sike said, "The hell with this," and emptied his gun into the man in front of him. They all howled in laughter. Woody swung his stick and it went right through the apparition, again the ungodly laughter. Dave slammed home his quick load and said, "I'm shooting at the snake, when I do everybody run."

The creature then opened its mouth exposing a hundred and eighty bright white teeth in a deathly grin. One of the avatars leapt at Dave and when it touched the living man it solidified and knocked him to the ground.

Starla looked at her mommy's face. Saw the despair, the tears of desperation in her eyes. She pushed out of Jessie's grasp and faced the giant serpent forty feet away.

"YOU"RE MEAN, GO AWAY!" When she yelled that, she stomped her right foot and brought her fists down to her sides. A large ripple ran through the air, like a single wave on a dead still pond. The men in black vanished. There was a look of puzzlement in the creature's eyes. Then every cell in its body separated as it burst into a cloud of mist that covered the rocks and trees, dripping in a black, viscose like liquid, spattering on the leaves. A small cloud of iridescent blue hung in the air where the creature had been. Starla was glowing with that same bright blue white light. After a bit the lights began to fade, and then disappeared.

Starla turned back to her mother and said, "Don't cry Mommy, it's all gone."

Jessie burst into a different kind of tears.

Epilogue

Jessie was shaking as she put Starla's shoes back on her feet. Woody peeled off his T shirt and wrapped it around Dwayne's wound. The bullet had grazed the side of his head, taking off the top of his ear, which bled like crazy. Dave Sike had approached the hole in the ground, slipping in the oily goo and peered down in. nothing but blackness.

Starla looked at her mother and asked, "Did I do a bad thing?"

Jessie pursed her lips, shook her head no, and held her daughter tight. She swallowed and then whispered, "No Honey, I think you saved all our lives."

Woody got Dwayne back on his feet and supported him, "I think we need to get back to the house," he said, "I really need to dress this wound."

Dave holstered his weapon as he walked back to the group, "You're right Woody, it's getting dark and it feels like rain, let's get started."

Lydia was overjoyed to see that Starla was with them and had the oil lamps burning. It was dusk and the rain started just as they crossed the back yard. Dwayne sat at the table as Woody did the job of putting on a proper bandage.

"Ya know Dwayne; you could go to one of them plastic surgeon fellers and become a half Vulcan. Ye'd be right in the new style of things, I saw a man on TV the other day that had his tongue split and his ears pointed." Woody was grinning.

"I'll just grow my hair a little longer, thank you very much," Dwayne replied.

"So tell me what happened," pleaded Lydia, "was Starla lost, did someone take her, what?"

Dave Sike was holding his coffee cup with both hands, "I'm still trying to figure things out. Jessie, you want to tell her?"

Lydia turned to Jessie who was still holding a now sleeping Starla. "Let me put her down, and then we can all tell the story."

Lydia sat and listened with her mouth hanging open, flabbergasted. "It was your mother? Oh my God, what was she trying to accomplish?"

"I think she wanted me to quit interfering with that damn gas well," Jessie said as she stared at the table, "she didn't know I was going to give it up. I don't think she would have hurt Starla, but she looked so crazy... I don't know."

"Well," said Dwayne, "that big ass snake thing took care of Patty, one bite, gone. I wish it had done that before she shot me though."

"I saw one of them fellers that was dancing around out there before. In the damn third bay, standing beside that wreck those girls got killed in," Woody spoke up, "scared the bejesus outta me."

"I saw a picture of one too," Dave said, "it was on the roll of film in the camera we found in that same car. We figured he was running beside the car just before it wrecked."

"So Dave," Jessie asked, "what do we do now, call the police, what?"

He looked at her, "Do you really want all this to get out? Starla will be the center of an investigation. Your Mother's name dragged into it, there won't be any secrets for long. How in the heck do we explain the monster?"

After much discussion it was decided that the men should go back out there where the cars were parked and take a real good look, try and find some answers for the thousand questions they had. Everybody found a place to sleep.

The next morning Dave, Woody, and a medicated Dwayne were looking at the cars. The oak that had crushed the front of the Lincoln posed a problem but Dwayne was sure he could cut it out of the way. They found Madeline's purse on the passenger seat. The Subaru yielded only an insurance card and a registration to a Phillip Quessling of Camp Hill, Pa. The overnight bag on the ground at the rear of the Continental held a partially used roll of designer duct tape. Dave Sike sat on the hood of the Subaru and began to put the puzzle together.

"We never saw Madeline Cornet but I must assume the two shots we first heard were for her and that she must have fell down that hole," Dave was speaking almost to himself, "why Patty wanted the child is obvious, but the governor's wife?"

"This is going to be a bigger investigation than anything Pennsylvania has seen before," Woody asserted, "there won't be no stone unturned."

"Unless, there ain't no stone to turn." Dwayne said, "With all the confusion from the earthquake and things all screwy, we might have enough time to make everything disappear." The three men looked at each other.

They first went out to the site where the hole was. They gathered up the spent brass and Patty's lower legs, her gun, and anything else they could find and threw it all down the hole. The night's rain had washed away the goo from the creature.

They worked together, cut the fallen tree off the Lincoln and towed both vehicles to the shop, stripped them, burnt the interiors and cut up the cars themselves with saws and the torch. The lock on the gate was replaced anew and the tracks leading back in were obliterated. Woody hauled the scrap metal from the cars over to Youngstown, Ohio and sold it. All accomplished in two days.

During those two days it was realized that both women were missing and could have been in the earthquake area in the time frame. The DAR of Titusville made the statement that they had not received a call from, nor seen either of the ladies. The State Police began their search. Woody had, had a terrible time finding a road out of the afflicted area and the searchers were hampered by the road and bridge damage as well. When they finally arrived at the Smith residence they learned only that Senator Lyons and Madeline Cornet were not, and had not been there. Not unusual given the family circumstances. The last trace of the women was a gas purchase made in Bellefonte.

The Governor made an anguished plea on television for the safe return of his wife and the Senator, begging anyone to come forward with any information. The FBI keyed in on the word "return" in his video and decided to investigate for a possible kidnapping. They turned over a lot of stones. Suspicion turned on the Governor himself. It didn't take long to uncover a few of Dougie's secrets.

He was surprised to find the federal agents at his door with a search warrant, 4:00 am on Sunday morning. He resigned two days later. Although he was never formally charged, his political ambitions were nullified. The fate of the two women remained a mystery.

The Marcellus Gas well survived and was producing a great volume of natural gas. Kerri Karson was lauded for her efforts and was named senior supervisor for all future wells in a three state area. The fact that the earthquake occurred at a crucial time in the fracking process was covered up by the well's success and well placed hush money paid to the media and scientific investigators.

Jessie and former Detective David Sike did a quiet internet search for Phillip Quessling. They discovered he was a ninety-two year old resident of a Camp Hill nursing home. He hadn't left the facility in six years. Dave concluded that it had been an obvious case of identity theft. No one ever noticed the camera that unknown man had placed in that tree, it's probably still there.

A couple months after all the commotion settled down, Jessie found out she was pregnant again and in the appropriate time Albinious William came into the world. Starla grew fast and remained a home schooled kid. She was taught not only the standard education but stressed kindness and patience in all things. She learned to control her emotions and thus her special abilities. She also began to test them too.

She adored her baby brother, even though by four he had become quite a little pest. It soon became apparent that he did not have any "extra" leanings and was just a normal little devil. Lydia became an integral part of the family. Though attractive, she never seemed to meet anyone that drew a special interest. She was devoted to her job.

They closed the business but Dwayne and Woody began restoring classic cars. Woody had gone back to the doctor a few months after the incident and found that his condition had vanished. After several tests the good doctor admitted his bafflement. Dave Sike noticed a renewed vigor and stamina, so did his happy wife.

After seven years had passed with no trace of the missing women they were both declared legally dead. Jessie inherited her mother's estate which was a good sum of money as the royalties had accumulated and drew interest. However, she was still legally bound by the agreement between her mother and the gas company. She thought it ironic that her mother had never seen the first check.

DNA can be a tricky thing. No one noticed the health of the Smith family as no one got sick, ever. Not only was Starla affected by the creature's mental abilities the thing that had kept it alive all those centuries was able to fuse in Starla's physiology and become spreadable. Whoever came into direct contact with her was infected. Hence, Woody's amazing recovery, and the continued good health of Dave Sike and his wife were simply chalked up to good fortune. Keeping Starla pretty much secluded from other people due to her special gifts had kept this unknown quality from spreading.

On her thirteenth birthday Starla told her dad she wanted a four-wheeler so she could drive around the many trails on their property. Dwayne said Okay, but she had to earn at least part of the money, if not half. This presented the young lady with a problem. How? She didn't get paid for chores, good grades, or watching her brother who was big enough now to watch himself.

She had been allowed to raise and sell sweet corn the last couple years but that would never be enough. Plus it was hard work. Then one evening she was watching the news about a charity carnival. One booth caught her eye and soon she was in business. The DNA was unknowingly getting spread to all of mankind. Until her mother found out what she was doing.

KISSES
OVER
4
SERVED
FREE
WIFI

Also by Robert Allen Pringle:

Trouble in Tionesta, how the world should end

Trafford Publishing

CPSIA information can be obtained at www.ICGtesting.com
Printed in the USA
BVOW02s2309110815

412911BV00001B/4/P

9 781634 905930